C000135173

A WITCH, HER CAT AND A HAUNTED HOUSE

A Tale of a Scarborough Witch, her Cat, and Ghosts.

By Graham A. Rhodes

First published 2023

Internet Kindle Edition 2023

Templar Publishing Scarborough N. Yorkshire

Conditions of Sale.

This book is sold subject to the condition that it shall not, by way of trade or otherwise, be lent, re-sold, hired out, or otherwise circulated without the publisher's prior consent, in any form of binding or cover other than that in which it is published.

Also available in the series of

Agnes the Scarborough Witch

A Witch, her Cat and a Pirate:
A story of a Scarborough witch, her cat and John Paul Jones

A Witch, her Cat and the Ship Wreckers:
A story of a Scarborough witch, her cat and ship wreckers and highwaymen.

A Witch her Cat and the Devil Dogs:
A story of a Scarborough witch and evil on the North Yorkshire Moors.

A Witch her Cat and A Viking Hoard:
A story of a Scarborough witch and the original Viking settlement of Skathaborg.

A Witch her Cat and The Whistler:
A Story of a Scarborough Witch, drug smuggling and spies in Robin Hoods Bay.

A Witch Her Cat and The Vampires:
A Story of a Scarborough Witch, vampires and vampire hunters on the North Yorkshire Moors.

A Witch Her Cat and The Moon People:
A Tale of a Scarborough Witch, her Cat, Gypsies
And Future Technology.

A Witch Her Cat and The Moon People:
A story of a Scarborough Witch, her Cat, Gypsies
And Future Technology.

A Witch, Her Cat and A Fire Demon:
A story of a Scarborough Witch and Pirates of the
Caribbean.

"A Witch Her Cat and A Revolution."
A story of A Scarborough Witch and the French
Revolution

"A Witch Her Cat and An Alchemist."
A story of a Scarborough Witch and stolen gold.

Catch up with Agnes at her web site
https://www.agnesthescarboroughwitch.com/

Dedication

This is the eleventh book of Agnes. As usual, it would have been impossible without the help and encouragement of the following people –

Yvonne, Jan for the editing, Jesse, Missy, Tubbs, Magenta, Anna (whose gig at the SJT started all this off) & all at Indigo Alley, Cellars and The Merchant, Dave, Northern Riots, the many fans and readers of Agnes who keep buying the books, and finally Ysanne (RIP).

Many of the streets and places mentioned in this book still exist in Scarborough's old town and up on the moors. They are well worth visiting. Once again I have taken the liberty of using the names of old Scarborough fishing families. I hope they don't mind their ancestors appearing here. However, the names and characters are all fictitious and should not be confused with anyone living or dead.

Character List

Agnes 21st & 18th Centuries
Our hero, an elderly lady who, as far as she knows, is over three hundred years old. She has no memory of who she is or where she came from. She lives in the same cottage in the Old Town of Scarborough in both centuries. She is either a wize woman or a witch, depending on who is telling the story. She is also a computer hacker.

Marmaduke 21st & 18th Centuries
Marmaduke lives with Agnes in her cottage. In the 21st century he is an old, grumpy, one-eared, one-eyed, sardine addicted cat. In the 18th century he is a one eyed, one eared, six-foot high ex-highwayman with very dangerous habits.

Andrew Marks 18th Century
The proprietor of the Chandlery situated on Scarborough's 18th century harbour side. Andrew is the eyes and ears of the small port. Nothing comes or goes in or out the port without him knowing about it, either legal or illegal.

Whitby John 18th Century
Ex-fisherman and landlord of The Three Mariners, Agnes' favourite public house.

Mrs. Whitby John (Nee Pateley) 18th Century
A Captain's widow and the new wife of Whitby
John. She is the broom that sweeps the Three
Mariners clean.

Salmon Martin 18th Century
A fisherman and regular of the Three Mariners.

Baccy Lad 18th Century
A young lad eager to please and helper at the
Three Mariners.

The Colonel-With-No-Name 18th Century
If you knew anymore he'd have to kill you.

The Gatekeeper
More than meets the eye.

George
A driver.

A Wally
A passenger.

Various Ghosts and Policemen
Extras.

A Witch, Her Cat and
A Haunted House.

Graham A. Rhodes.

Chapter One.

It was there, the white face at the window. Its eyes were dark shadows and the watchers hidden in the bushes felt it was looking directly at them. They nudged each other. One of them turned from the image he was filming on his mobile phone and winked at the other. This was why they had spent four consecutive cold and uncomfortable nights waiting for. Despite the inconvenience of peering out of a large rhododendron bush they had brought along two small camping stools and a flask of coffee, liberally laced with whisky. It was just as it had been described to them earlier in the week. The search had started by an e-mail sent to the Scarborough Paranormal Society claiming a sighting had been recorded by a local man who had seen the face on more than one occasion whilst walking his dog. Judging by the state of the abandoned garden his wasn't the only dog that used the place as a toilet. "Bob Martins Alley!" one of them had called it as he scraped the offending mess off his boot on the first night of their vigil. They had been more careful on the second and third nights and wore small strap-on headlamps to pick their way to their hiding place. The face disappeared and the mobile phone was switched off. The two of them glanced at each other.

"Come on!" One of them said.

Once out of the darkness of their hiding place the path to the building was illuminated by the thin moonlight peering from above the clouds. It shone down on a small cottage almost hidden by invasive shrubbery and neglect. The roof was littered by broken and cracked roof tiles through which skeletal beams could be seen. It looked beyond repair. The windows on the ground floor were broken as was the door that hung half open off its hinges allowing access to the numerous homeless vagrants that had used the place as a shelter. Graffiti across the walls impinged the reputation of someone called Mandy. Someone else had tried to illustrate a futuristic scene with aerosol paint cans but had not made a very good job of it.

Carefully they entered being aware of dodgy floorboards and deep cellars. Once inside the smell made them wince. It was as if every fox for miles around had made a special journey just to urinate in the house. Carefully avoiding a pile of broken bottles and discarded needles they moved to the staircase. Their lights shone as they gingerly climbed the shaking stairs, testing each step as they
14

moved upwards. When they reached the landing they paused to find their bearings. They were facing the rear of the house so the face in the window must have appeared in the room to their left. They tiptoed across the landing. As they reached the door it silently opened, not fully, just enough to cause curiosity, as if the movement on the landing had caused the old timbers to shift. They looked at each other, counted three on their fingers and rushed forward. The door flew open as they burst into the room. It was deserted. Ideally they hope to find some local kid who didn't like dog walkers and was hiding in there with a scary mask. Their bravado told them they wanted to find actual proof of a ghost that they could take back to amaze the other members of their society. One of them shone his light onto the floor by the window where the apparition had appeared. There was nothing but dirt debris and bird droppings. He looked out of the window into the street and blinked. He nudged his friend.

"Wrong room!" he said.

They returned to the landing. There was only one other door. The pushed it forward. It creaked and groaned as it reluctantly opened, but open it did. They looked into the room. There was the window. As they looked on the floor for any footprints they
15

were unaware of a black shape that oozed up from the floorboards appearing behind them, like some grotesque shadow. It filled the room behind them, then like a cloud of soot, it fell over the two young men. When the soot stopped falling and settled on the floor the two men had vanished.

Chapter Two

Agnes was walking back from the corner shop with her "bag for life" half filled with cut price tins of sardines and a loaf of bread. She would have ordered it via the internet but she felt it did her good to get out and about now and again. Well that wasn't quite right, she was fit enough. She needed to get out and about to make sure that the neighbours could see that she was alive and well. For some reason beyond her the idea of an old lady living by herself seemed to be a matter of concern for all and sundry. From the woman from Age Concern, to her nosy neighbour, to the milkman, (and yes, despite the fact she could buy litres of the stuff at half the price from the local supermarket, she still used the services of an old fashioned milkman. She believed in buying local.).

"A pity about those two young men wasn't it!" The voice across the narrow street brought her back to the present. She lifted her head. It was the nosy neighbour. Agnes smiled and nodded. She had no idea what the woman was talking about.

"The police can't find a trace. Everyone's saying the ghost must have got them. They reckon it's on
17

telly tonight. Someone saw that woman from Look North and a cameraman hanging around this morning."

Agnes smiled again. She still had no idea of what the woman was talking about. Much to her relief she had reached her front door. As she opened it she turned to the woman. "I'm sure they'll turn up. Look North? I'll make a point of watching."

Not wanting to appear rude she exchanged a couple more pleasantries before extracting herself from the conversation and closed the door behind her.

She dropped her shopping in the living room and sat in front of her computer. Without the need to switch it on she moved her hand and the latest on-line edition of the Scarborough News flashed up in front of her.

"I really must pay more attention to local events!" she said to herself as she skimmed the headlines. It was the second story, the lead one being how the current Lord Mayor had been attacked by a seagull that had tried to steal his gold chain of office.

She read on "Police hunt missing ghost hunters.", was the next headline. She read the copy. Two men from the Scarborough Paranormal Society had vanished. The last anyone had seen of them was a sighting by a dog walker who saw them at the rear of an old cottage in a small street in Scarborough's old town. There was a photograph of the cottage. She recognised it. It was tucked away in one of the old town's smaller streets called Tuthill. She looked at the photograph of the bulding and remembered when it was a smart little cottage with a well kept garden, a little patch of green trimmed by a flower bed with a sea view that overlooked the harbour. She smiled, that was a long time ago now, when the cottage was owned by a sea captain, then a merchant, then....she forgot. There had been so many owners over the years, so many lives that came and went. There again, it was the same for all the houses in the old town. People came and went, that's life.

She read on. At first no one had noticed their disappearance until one of them didn't turn up for work. Then someone made enquiries, friends were consulted, members of the Society questioned. No one had seen the two for at least three days. She checked the date on the article. It was current. Her curiosity was aroused, she just had to know more. She checked the time and flicked her finger. Her television came on. She waited a while until Look North began. It was their lead story. The person in
19

the studio mentioned a few details concerning the disappearance and then cut to a woman presenter who was standing in the rear garden of the cottage. She went into more details and then interviewed the dog walker who, being unused to appearing on the television, muttered something about seeing them a few evenings ago. They then turned to a second interviewee, a woman police inspector who pointed out that the investigation was on-going and that foul play wasn't suspected, and who asked members of the public for any information before ending with the message that there was no need for the public to be worried and if the two missing men were watching would they please get in touch with the Scarborough Police. A number flashed on the screen and the presenter passed the viewers back to the studio, and problems with traffic congestion on the A64.

Now, not only was Agnes's curiosity aroused, it was dancing a jig in the middle of her living room. She had to know more. She had to have a look at the building for herself. She realised that the sight of an elderly lady climbing all over a suspected crime scene probably wouldn't do her reputation any good so she did what she always did. She fetched her scrying bowl. When it was full of water she sprinkled some herbs and spices over its surface and then passed her hand over it. An image appeared. She was looking down on the old cottage. Sure enough a community policeman stood at the front and at the rear. She peered deeper into the garden and moved her hand once more. The image clouded and then cleared. She was looking down on the same scene but now she could see two men hiding in the overgrown rhododendron bush. She watched as they crept out of their cover and entered the building. She moved her hand once more and saw the view from inside the house. She watched as the two headlights bobbed up and down as they climbed the staircase. She watched as they entered an upstairs room, realised their mistake and entered the second. Then she blinked. One moment they were there, the next they had vanished. She moved her hand and replayed the scene. It happened again. Then she clicked her fingers and the images changed into slow motion. If it had been a video she would have played it frame by frame. As it was she slowed it down even further. Each time it was the same, one moment they were there, the next they had disappeared. There was no blur, no half-there half-gone, no fading away, just there, not there. She sat back.

"Now that's a bit of a puzzle!" she thought.
She looked at the image once more. This time she probed the room with all her senses. She sniffed.

Nothing. She moved her hand and was looking down at the cottage and the two community policemen again.

"Well it wasn't magic!" she said to herself and added. "But if it wasn't magic what was it?" She needed to take a closer look.

She marched out of her sitting room and into the kitchen where the old ginger cat was sleeping on her dishwasher. Agnes liked her dishwasher, it was one of the benefits of 21st century life. She gave it a fond pat which set it off on one of its cycles and woke the cat up. It opened its one good eye and gave her a long hard stare.

"Just popping out for minute!" she said and stepped into her backyard. The cat lifted its head and looked out of the window. The air around Agnes shimmered and a seagull rose into the evening sky.

It flew over a number of houses before settling on the chimney of the small derelict cottage. The two police were still standing at the front and rear of the building. Further down the street a small group of curious youths had gathered. From the cans of beer and strong lager clutched in their hands Agnes could see their plans of using the cottage for a secret drinking den had been thwarted. Instead they contented themselves by making loud and disparaging comments aimed at the policeman until he stepped forward and told them to move on. Sulkily they moved a few yards down the street muttering to themselves. No one saw the air on top of the building shimmer and no one saw a large rat sniff the air before scampering down the chimney. She emerged inside the room where the two men had vanished. The rat scampered around the edges of the room sniffing the air and snuffling at the floorboards. Still she found nothing that could explain their disappearance. The air shimmered once again and Agnes stood in the far corner.

She moved her hand and patterns of footprints appeared among the dust and dirt on the floorboards. It took her some while to sort out the ones left by the young men from those left by members of the North Yorkshire Police. When she did separate them she still found nothing. The footprints walked into the room and just stopped. She tried every spell and trick she could think of but nothing came to light. She sighed and then glanced out of the window, which was unfortunate because one of the policemen just happened to be looking up at the time. There was a shout from below and his colleague appeared. One pointed at the window whilst the other began speaking on his

23

radio. The air shimmered and the rat scampered across the floor and up the chimney. As a seagull rose from the roof of the cottage the sound of a police car siren could be heard in the distance. Agnes marched from the backyard into the kitchen, picked up the cat and walked down into her cellar. Halfway down the steps she turned and stepped through a door that wasn't there and entered her cellar in the 18th century. Now instead of Agnes and her cat Agnes was standing with a six foot tall, ginger haired, one eyed, ex-highwayman. Marmaduke looked at her as he patted the hair behind his head and tried to lick his own shoulder. Agnes said nothing. It always took Marmaduke a few seconds to adjust from being a cat to becoming a human. Well, as much a human as a half-cat, half-human can be. He paused from washing himself and looked at Agnes.

"Problems?" he asked.

Agnes shrugged. "I'm not sure. I need to have a think."

Marmaduke nodded. He knew well enough that Agnes did some of her best thinking in the Three Mariners with a not so small glass of brandy. He left the cellar and began to put on his coat.

Fifteen minutes later Agnes was sitting in her favourite chair at the side of the fireplace in the bar of the small, bright bar room with a glass of brandy in her hand. Marmaduke glanced around the room, all the regulars were there. Salmon Martin was telling a far-fetched tale of sea monsters to an enthralled audience of fishermen and dockworkers. Baccy Lad stood leaning on the bar. Marmaduke saw he still wore his hair braided and two gold rings were hanging from his ears. Ever since his adventure with Agnes he had looked more and more like a pirate. Each to their own he thought.

Behind the bar Whitby John stood polishing a glass. His wife stood next to him, she was the person responsible for changing the little inn from a dark, dingy, smoke filled room into a bright cheerful place where drinkers could actually see what they were drinking, and who they were talking to. Agnes said nothing but stared into the fireplace watching the flames dance and glow. Her attention was suddenly attracted by two men she didn't recognise. By their clothing she could tell they weren't from the fishing community. She sniffed. There was a faint smell of wood shavings, brick dust and damp mortar about them. She nodded to herself. They were builders. She attuned herself to their conversation. They were talking about some timber that had been delivered to them that morning. It seemed they weren't over impressed with its quality.

"Too new. It should have been seasoned!" One observed.
The other shook his head. "Good enough for the job in hand."

Agnes was intrigued. She carried on listening.

"It's a decent enough little house. Only been standing for sixty odd years. No need to replace them timbers and floorboards."

The other man gave a short bark like laugh. "At least we'll get a decent price for the stuff we've pulled out!"

Agnes couldn't help herself. She stood up and moved next to them. As she spoke she gave them both one of her special looks. "Excuse me but I couldn't help overhearing. Whereabouts are you working?"

The two builders looked at the elderly lady. Instead of telling her to mind her own business they found themselves engaged in a conversation where they were about to divulge their life stories, or they would have done if the lady had not directed the
26

conversation towards the job they were engaged upon. They told her it was a small cottage at the end of a small lane, deep inside the Old Town. Agnes felt a little tingle run down her spine as she realised she was talking to the two builders who had laid the floorboards that, less than an hour ago and over three hundred years in the future, she had walked over.

"Why are you refitting the cottage?" She asked. The two builders looked at each other. Neither of them spoke. Agnes gave them another of her special looks.

One of the men looked around the bar, making sure they weren't being overheard. "Bloke that owns it reckons the place is cursed. He's had nothing but bad luck ever since he bought the place."

The second leant forward until he was almost speaking into Agnes's ear. "Reckons its haunted!" He stood up, crossed himself and took a gulp of his drink.

Agnes nodded and allowed the conversation to revert to their normal everyday lives and concerns. They told her they had been brought into the Old Town from nearby Falsgrave and that they had worked for the owner before on another of his properties. He had been pleased with their work and hired them again. Life in the 18th century was very similar to life in the 21st century. If you found a good reliable builder you stuck with him.

She smiled, bade them a goodnight and flicked her finger. The two men continued talking among themselves, unaware of the conversation they had just had and unaware that their tankards had been replenished.

She walked across to the bar and nodded at Whitby John who put his polishing cloth down and leant across the bar to listen to her.

"What do you know about that cottage that's being rebuilt down Tuthill?"

Whitby John shrugged. "Not much. The owner is some retired army chap. He has a cousin up in Sandside somewhere. Moved in a year ago now."

Agnes lowered her voice. "Rumour has it the place is haunted!"

Whitby John laughed. "Don't tell me you've been listening to one of Salmon Martins daft stories."

"So it's untrue then." She said.

A serious look crossed Whitby John's face. "I'm not saying it is and not saying it isn't. In my experience just because somewhere gets a reputation for something people are always keen to blame it on ghosts or some superstitious clap trap."

He suddenly remembered who he was talking to and his face reddened. "Present company excepted. No offence Agnes!"

She smiled. "None taken, but why has it a reputation? I've never heard anything."

Whitby John scratched his head. "It would have been a while ago now. Someone hung himself in there. Decent bloke. From what I remember he was an ex-soldier. Seen action somewhere or other, can't remember where. Anyway he hadn't been seen for a day or so when his housekeeper found him hanging from a beam in his own bedroom. Gave her a nasty shock I can tell you."

Agnes settled herself at the bar. She had a feeling there was more. She was right. Whitby John continued.

"Then there was that salesman. Sold hardware for a company in York I think."

"What happened to him?" Agnes said feeling she knew the answer already.

Whitby John shook his head. "No one knows. He disappeared overnight. Wasn't hide nor hair of him ever seen again. Mind you the word was that he was working some sort of fiddle and fled afore he were found out!"

Agnes nodded. The time for thinking was over. She drained her glass, said goodnight to her host, collected Marmaduke and returned home explaining her conversations along the way.

When they were home Agnes looked at Marmaduke. "I'm going back to the 21st century. It would be useful if you could walk down Tuthill. Have a look at the work the builders are doing. Have a friendly chat with them and see what you can find out, then have a chat with the neighbours."

Marmaduke raised the eyebrow over his one good eye. "What am I looking for?"

Agnes shrugged. "Anything you can find out really."

Marmaduke reached for his coat. Agnes gave him a look. "The morning will do!" She said. He replaced his coat behind the door and settled down in front of the fire. Agnes marched downstairs and into her cellar.

The first thing she did back in the 21st century was to wave her hand and fire up her computer. Despite it being only a few hours since she had seen the news she checked both the Scarborough News and the BBC North websites to see if there had been and further developments. There hadn't.

Then she moved her finger and brought up the appropriate page of Google Earth. The image had been taken a couple of years previously, when the rear of the property hadn't been so overgrown. Nothing caught her attention. She wriggled her finger a bit more and as Google began a long and very detailed search she went off the make herself a cup of Mr Tetley's very fine tea.

When she returned she checked the screen and clicked a finger. Her printer sprang into life. When it had finished she had a pile of paperwork that traced the deeds of the Tuthill property all the way back to its first owner.

Once she had read them she clicked her finger once again and brought up all the available details and records of the previous owners. She began browsing through a mountain of old deeds, old census records, old leases and death certificates. It took her the best part of the night but by the time she had finished she had a complete record of every owner and occupant since the property had been built until the late 20th century when it fell derelict. It made for interesting reading. Since its construction the property had been owned by twenty people of which five had committed suicide and six disappeared without trace.

She sat back in her chair. Including the two ghost hunters, that made eight people who had disappeared over three hundred years. Given that length of time she supposed it wasn't an unusual statistic. Agnes was well aware the people disappeared for any number of reasons. It wasn't as rare as people imagined. Five suicides was not unusual. However put them all together in one small cottage and then a red light began to flash. Taken over the years each event was just a small tragedy or a little mystery but put it all together and look at the bigger picture and something didn't seem right. Agnes believed in the big picture. You do when you're over three hundred years old. At that age big pictures don't seem so big. What puzzled her was that in all that time she had never become aware of any of the suicides or disappearances. Each one had passed her by. She racked her memory. Vague memories of people and faces came and went. Snatches of past conversations rose and fell. At the time people had talked, some had asked questions, but no one had listened. The each event was passed over for newer news, newer gossip and in time it became forgotten.

As dawn broke outside Agnes sat thinking of the forgotten people. Then she gave a slight shrug of her shoulders. She refused to beat herself up about it. What happened had happened. It was in the past and there was nothing she could do about it. Now it had caught her attention was the right time to do something about it. The past was the past, but the future was unwritten. She decided to take a walk past the house and wander down to the pier. Perhaps pop into the Look Out cafe and enjoy one of their excellent breakfasts. She hated thinking on an empty stomach. She checked the time. It was six thirty. The cafe would be open as it catered not only for tourists but also the fishermen, market workers and other harbour side workers.

As she walked past the house in Tuthill she noticed that sometime in the night the police guard had

33

changed. She was in luck as she recognised one of them. She had been born two streets away and as a small child he had suffered from severe asthma. Despite medications and treatments offered by the NHS it hadn't shifted. That was until Agnes had been consulted. She had mixed up a special potion and instructed the worried mother to rub it onto the child's front and back every night for a month. The mother did as instructed and the child was cured. The doctors and medics claimed that the child must have grown out of her condition. Agnes and the child's mother knew better.

She approached the policewoman with a smile and a wave. The policewoman saw her approaching. "You're up and about early Agnes!" She remarked.

"I just fancied breakfast on the pier!" Agnes replied.

The policewoman looked at her watch. "Lucky you. I'm stuck here for another three hours. I could use a cuppa!"

"How about a bacon sandwich?" Agnes offered. The policewoman nodded. "I'll bring you one up. What about your friend around the back?"

The policewoman looked around and seeing that no one else was around bent down to Agnes. "You hang on here and I'll go and ask him!"

She was gone longer than Agnes expected. When she reappeared she was shaking her head and speaking into her radio. Agnes waited until she had finished.

The policewoman clicked off her radio and looked at Agnes. "He's not there. He was meant to be guarding the rear door that leads into the garden. I looked everywhere. There's no sign of him!"

"Did you look inside?" Agnes asked.

The policewoman looked around her and shook her head. "Strict instructions not to pass the tape without permission." She replied and added, "Anyway the doors still sealed!"

Agnes wasn't stupid enough to ask her if she had checked the bushes and the garden. She knew she had. The policewoman's radio burst into life and Agnes took a step backwards. As the policewoman answered the many questions that were being thrown at her Agnes allowed her senses to drift over the house and the back garden. She found a trace of something. There was a slight glow by the back door where the policeman must have been standing. She concentrated. The glow shifted to one of the back windows and into the downstairs room where it vanished.

Then policewoman turned off her radio. "Someone will be along in a minute. They'll want to ask questions so if I were you I'd slip away quietly. I'll just say you passed by on your way to the cafe. We won't mention bacon sandwiches!"

Agnes nodded and walked down Tuthill, but instead of heading down to the harbour she turned back up Princess Street and returned to her house where she picked up her scrying bowl. Breakfast could wait, she thought to herself.

After she had filled the bowl with water and sprinkled her mixture of herbs and spices onto its surface she passed her hand over it. As it cleared she saw three police cars edge their way down the tiny street and both uniformed and plain clothes officers climbed out and swarmed over the building and garden. The policewoman was led to a car where she made her statement.

Agnes followed the police as they entered the building and moved from room to room examining every nook and cranny for a sign of their missing
36

colleague. There was no trace to be found. They moved upstairs and entered the second bedroom, again they found nothing. Then they came to the first bedroom, the one where the young men had vanished. As they approached the open door it sudden slammed shut in their faces. One of them reached out and grabbed the door knob. He twisted it, but the door still wouldn't open. He pushed it with his shoulder. It didn't move. His colleagues lent their weight and pushed. It still held firm.

Agnes lowered her hand over the bowl and spread her fingers. There was no trace of magic. She crooked her little finger and felt something revisiting. It was only slight but it was there. She pushed. It pushed back. She pushed a bit harder. The water in the scrying bowl began to move. Tiny ripples appeared moving from the middle to the edge. She moved a second finger and the door flew open spilling the policemen into the room. They remained on their feet more by good luck than by good management. Once inside they regained their equilibrium and took a couple of steps forward. Then they stopped. Lying on the floor, at the edge of the room was the missing policeman's radio. She moved her hand and the vision clouded. It cleared once more to reveal the image of the cottage two hours earlier. She could see the policeman standing in the garden when suddenly he looked up. Agnes followed his gaze. There in the upstairs window was a face. It was white, its eyes were hidden in deep shadow, its mouth moved. It seemed to be saying "Help me, help me". Silently it mouthed the words again and again. She watched as the policeman moved forwards and entered the building by the downstairs window. She watched as he ran up the stairs and straight into the room pulling out his radio. Halfway across the room he seemed to just disappear. All that could be seen was his radio falling to the ground and bouncing on the bare floorboards settling just under the window.

Agnes moved her hand and the vision cleared. She sat back. The policeman had vanished just like the others. That would mean more policemen. They would do a fingertip examination of the area. They would do house to house enquiries. They would bring in some expert forensic investigators, and they would discover nothing. She knew that because she knew there was nothing to find.

Of course the press would be there in their droves. Every hotel room and boarding house would be full of reporters from the national press. In a matter of hours the streets of the Old Town would be full of cables and lights and presenters doing pieces to camera. Look North would hardly get near to the place. She gave a little shudder. The last thing she needed were a lot of curious journalists asking awkward questions. She scooped up all the information she had gathered, cast a spell over her computer and her front door and walked down into the cellar and through the door that wasn't there. When she returned to the 18th century the house was deserted. Marmaduke must have gone out early. She cleared the table in the front room and spread the papers out before her, carefully placing all the information about the previous owners in chronological order, starting with the 21st century and working backwards. She sat and studied them. Then she separated out the owners or occupants who had died there. Finally she pulled out a pile of the ones who had disappeared. She looked at the papers. There was no obvious pattern. She leant back and gave the matter some more thought. Did the events have to be linked? Perhaps everything was random. She shook her head. Of course there was a link. The house itself was the link. She looked at the piles of papers once more. She had some facts, but not all of them. She was certain there was some clue there, but for the life of her she couldn't find it. She decided to do some investigating of her own. She stood up, placed a woollen shawl around her shoulders and stepped out into the bright 18th century September morning.

As she turned into the narrow passageway that led from Princess Street into Tuthill she came across Mrs Stokes scuttling towards her with her basket in her hand. The woman stopped and greeted Agnes who made pleasant comments about the day and asked after her family. All was well. The fishing was good and the weather fair, two very important things if your family depended on the fishing. Agnes paused the conversation as she looked down the lane.

"How's the building work going on?" She asked.

Mrs Stokes shook her head. "Don't know what's going on. Can't make head nor tail of it. Perfectly good little house and they're ripping it apart and rebuilding it from the inside." She looked around her and lowered her voice. "If you ask me that fellow that owns it has more money than sense."

"Who is he?" Agnes asked. She knew already. She had read the name on the deeds but itys always nice to have your research confirmed.

"I heard he's a retired army chaplain. Came from somewhere down south. I think he knows the Commander of the Garrison, they served together in the American War."

Now that was one bit of information she didn't know. "I don't supposed you know where he is?" Mrs Stokes shook her head. "I don't know but by the liberties the builders are taking with the old timbers I would hazard a guess he's well away!" Agnes raised an eyebrow as the woman continued. "They've set up a wood yard at the back. Selling it off to anyone who'd have it. I bet that money's not going into the pocket of the owner!"

Agnes nodded. From what had been said before it seemed all above board. She let out a strange half laugh at her own bad pun. The woman gave her a slight frown, she didn't regard the resale of used timber a suitable subject for humour. Recycling wasn't that important on the 18th century, although she knew a number of the ship builders down on the harbour side who would benefit from cheap timber.

The two women commented on the weather before saying their polite goodbyes and Agnes continued her walk down Tuthill. Further down the street she spotted Marmaduke lounging casually against a wall.

"Anything?" She asked.

41

Marmaduke shook his head. "Nothing. The neighbours seem as mystified as everyone else why the work is being done. The story is that someone bought it, moved in, and left after a few months. The next thing anyone knows is the builders arrive and start their working."

Agnes glanced at the house. Behind the open windows she could see the workmen moving around. "I don't suppose anyone has mentioned seeing a white ghostly face at an upstairs window?"

Marmaduke shook his head.

"Keep watching!" She said and wandered back up Tuthill.

Thirty minutes later she was being shown into the office of the Commander of the Scarborough Garrison. He stood up as she entered the room.

"Good day madam. I trust you and your...." he paused. He had almost said the word cat!

"Marmaduke!" Agnes said.

The Commander harrumphed."Yes of course, Marmaduke. I trust you are both well?"

"Thank you Commander we are as fine as I hope you and your command are. I have come to enquire about a mutual acquaintance."

The Commander bade her to sit and pulled a chair up to his desk before sitting down. "Mutual acquaintance you say? Who would that be?"

"The retired army chaplain who's bought a house down in Tuthill."

The Commander thought for a few seconds and then grinned. "Oh, Old Pinky! Yes Pinky Deconsfield. Served with him in America you know. Damn fine fellow, damn fine chaplain don't you know!"

Agnes prevented herself from saying that she didn't know, that was why she was asking, but she knew from experience that the Commander had no concept of irony, so she didn't. Instead she smiled. "I don't suppose you know where he is?"

The Commander gave another harrumph and played with the end of his moustache as he thought. When he closed his eyes Agnes was afraid that he'd fallen asleep. Then he grunted.

"York! That's it I remember now. He left a month ago. He had some business to attend to at the Garrison there. Something about his pension I believe. Then he mentioned something about visiting the Minster. He had an appointment with someone connected with the church. Some cannon or priest or something. No idea why. Probably needed some advice." He coughed, harrumphed again and added. "Of the religious sort!"

Agnes cocked her head. "Now why would he be needing any advice. I thought he had retired?"

The Colonel nodded vigorously. "That's why his first port of call was the army paymaster. Sorting out his pension." He paused and looked out of the window across the inner aspect of the Castle and its Norman tower. Agnes remained silent.
"We had dinner before he went. Over the brandy he made a bit of a confession. The chap told me he was losing his religion. Told me something had happened that made him question the whole bally thing!"

"What did you say to him?" Agnes asked.

The Colonel let out another harrumph. "Told him to pull himself together. Told him he had done damn fine service to his regiment, his King and his God."

Agnes thought for a moment before speaking. "I suppose the stuff you see on the battlefield is enough to make anyone question their faith!" "The Colonel shook his head. "I don't think it had anything to do with the army, of the battles he saw. It was something that happened after he came here, to Scarborough. I told him that he was probably just missing the army, missing the routine and the discipline. Happens to many chaps, once you're out in the world you have time to think. That's the good thing about the army, don't have time to think!"

Agnes didn't say anything. She let the comment hang in the air. "What rank did he leave with?"

The Commander thought for a few seconds. "Captain I believe. Captain George Deaconsfield, Army Chaplain."

Agnes nodded and rose from her chair offering her hand out for the Commander to shake. "Thank you Commander. As usual your knowledge has been of great assistance."

The Commander puffed out his chest."Anything to oblige Agnes, you know me!"

He stood and strode across the room to open the door for her. As she left she turned. "I forgot, why did you call him Pinky?"
The Commander barked out a laugh. "The fellow blushed easily. He was always easily offended. Mutter a rude word in his company and his face would redden. He laughed again. "Pinky, jolly good name for him."

Agnes left him to relive his memories and returned to her house where she rummaged through her papers until she found the deeds and information she had gathered. She looked up information on Captain Deaconsfield. The first thing she came across was his death certificate. She looked at the date and smiled. The man would live for a good few years yet. He would die of old age in his own bed. She checked the address, it wasn't in the house in Tuthill. She checked the deeds again. He would only own the house for another year then he would sell it and move to a house in the more fashionable Ramshill part of town. She put the papers down. She needed to talk with this ex-army chaplain and she knew someone in York that could help her trace the man.

Chapter Three.

That night the air shimmered and an owl took off from between the roofs of the Old Town. As it rose in the air it flapped its wings. The air around it blurred and the owl faded into the evening darkness.

Early next morning an elderly lady walked up to the main gate of the York Garrison. Politely she drew the attention of one of the guards and whispered something into his ear. He stopped and looked at the woman who rummaged in her pocket and drew out a round ivory token. The guard examined it and without a word, turned and marched away to his commanding officer. Ten minutes later Agnes was being ushered into an office deep within the garrison. As she entered the room she gave a smile.

The Colonel-with-no-name stood up and put his hand out in greeting. "Good to see you again Agnes. How can we help?"

Agnes sat down and told the man her story. The whole story, even the future bits. She had learnt that if you were to share secrets, the best people to

share those secrets with were the people who held
bigger secrets, and no one in England held more
secrets than the Head of the Government Security,
answerable only to King George himself. The
Colonel-with-no-name listened patiently. When
Agnes stopped talking he asked a question.
"Do you think it really is a ghost?"

Agnes gave a shrug. "I've no idea. I do know it
isn't magic!"

The Colonel shook his head. "It's not just your
magic you know about, perhaps a ghost is just a
different kind of magic!"

Before she answered him Agnes stopped to think.
The man could be right. Perhaps ghosts, spirits and
poltergeists were just another kind of magic. A
type no one had yet discovered."

"Well it's an idea!" She replied.

"Just an idea." The Colonel repeated with a
twinkle in his eye and then added. "I take it you
want me to track down this Deaconsfield feller."
Agnes nodded. "I would appreciate an introduction
to the gentleman!"

The Colonel scribbled out a note, sifted sand over

the wet ink and rang a bell. A soldier entered the room and the Colonel handed him the folded paper. Exchanging salutes the soldier turned and left to room.

"Breakfast?" The Colonel asked. Agnes nodded.

They had barely finished the meal before the soldier returned. He handed the paper to the Colonel who glanced at it and passed it onto Agnes. She unfolded it to reveal and name and an address. It simply read. Captain George Deaconsfield. C/O The Old Starr Inn, Stonegate York. She refolded the paper and dropped it into her pocket.

"Thank you!" She said.

"You will let me know how things develop?" The Colonel asked.

Agnes smiled. "Of course. Although you are aware there is nothing I can do about things that are about to happen."

The Colonel raised his head and looked at Agnes, she shrugged. "At least not until the year 2024."

The Colonels expression hardened slightly. "What about the people yet to disappear, to hang themselves?"

A sad expression crossed Agnes's face, as if a dark cloud had crossed over her own private sun. "What will happen will happen. The clues I seek are here in this time. Those clues are the key to stopping whatever is happening three hundred years hence."

The Colonel nodded. "Can't change history eh?" Agnes nodded in agreement and gave a little smile."But you can give a slight jolt now and again!"

The Colonel smiled. "We do what we can!"

Agnes nodded. "You more than others!"

The Colonel shrugged. "Sometimes I think peace is more difficult to wage than war. At least in times of war we know who the enemy is!"

Agnes remembered that the war in the American Colonies had ended. King George had lost and the Americans were now organising themselves into an independent country under a man called Washington.

At that moment there was another knock on the door. The Colonel granted entrance and another soldier marched in and handed him another piece of paper. The Colonel unfolded it and read its contents. He looked up at Agnes.

"It seems our man is on the move. He ate a hearty breakfast in the Old Star and walked down Stonegate to the Minster where he met a certain gentleman of the cloth who led him into the Chapter House where they had a secret meeting."

He looked up at Agnes. "It should prove interesting. I have heard of the man he is meeting. He is the Archbishop of York's exorcist."

Agnes smiled. "So the man knows the house is haunted and is trying to do something about it."

"It seems that way." The Colonel replied.

Agnes stood up. "It's time I was going. I'll try to waylay the man as he leaves the Minster. Colonel, as always it has been a pleasure."

The Colonel smiled as he shook her hand. "The pleasure has been all mine. A carriage is waiting for you at the gatehouse. It is yours for as long as you need it."

Agnes thanked him and a soldier escorted her through the building and led her to a waiting carriage. She felt quite important as she was driven from Fulford down into York, through the City Bar and right up to the front door of the Minster.

After she had been helped out she stood on the steps of the Minster whilst the driver arranged to position himself at the other side of the road where he would wait for her. She had no idea of where she was going next. At the back of her mind was a meeting and then a return to Scarborough, but having a carriage at her disposal was such a novelty that she didn't want it to end.

She turned and entered the Minster. As she walked down the length of the nave she looked up at the colourful stained glass windows. It was a very impressive building. She found the Chapter House where she was approached by a member of the Minster Clergy who asked her business. She told him she was hoping to see Captain Deaconsfield as he left his meeting. Despite her age the man was obviously uneasy speaking to an unaccompanied female. He blustered and harrumphed. He was about to suggest she waited elsewhere when the door opened and a tall gentleman dressed in a long black frock coat emerged. He halted when he found his progress stopped by two people. Agnes took the initiative.

"Captain Deaconsfield." She held out her hand. "A pleasure to meet you. We have a mutual acquaintance in the Commander of the Scarborough Garrison." As she spoke she gave him one of her special looks. The man held out his hand. It was then Agnes recognised the appropriateness of the man's nickname. As he shook her hand his face turned bright red.

Agnes led the man out of the Chapter House and away from the preying eyes of the Minster Clergy. As she walked him down the nave she had an idea. "Sir, I know this is most unusual but I do need a conversation with you about your Scarborough residence. I have a carriage waiting. Come take a drive with me and we will talk about your residence as we view the pleasant aspects of this fine city."

Captain Deaconsfield had no idea why he accepted the invitation from this peculiar looking lady. All he knew was that he was being escorted out of the Minster, across the road and was seated in the back of a rather fine carriage. Once she had settled herself Agnes leaned out of the window and addressed the driver.

53

"I need to talk to this gentleman, if you would be as so kind as to take us a drive around the city. Take your time as it might prove a long conversation."

As the carriage set off at a slow pace Agnes settled back and addressed her passenger. "Sir as I said I am acquainted with the Commander. Indeed it was he who suggested that I seek you here in York."

Captain Deaconsfield said nothing. He could only feel himself reddening. He looked right and left. Outside the streets of York were slowly passing by. Suddenly he felt a sense of calm surround him. He relaxed. Agnes stopped moving her finger as the man's face returned to its normal colour. She came straight to the point.

"Captain, I could broach this subject in any number of ways. I could say your neighbours in Tuthill are concerned about you. They wonder why you are rebuilding a perfectly good property. I could say that the Commander has shown concern. But I know the answer."

She paused for dramatic effect. The man said nothing but stared straight ahead. She continued. "You have employed builders to alter your house. You have consulted with the exorcist of the
54

Archbishop of York. I put it to you Sir that you believe the house to be haunted."

Sometimes she could be too direct she told herself as she pulled out her small bottle of smelling salts and wafted it under the Captains nose. His eyes fluttered and she sat back as he emerged from his faint.

In the next few minutes it was difficult to say who was the most apologetic, the Captain for fainting, or Agnes for making him faint in the first place. She glanced out of the window and noticed a coffee house. A good dose of caffeine would probably do the man some good. She banged her fist on the inner wall and the carriage eased to a stop.

Fortified by a pot of very strong coffee and a twitch from Agnes's finger the man told his story. At first he had been happy in the house, then he had heard the noises. Initially he had put it down to the house itself and its shifting timbers. Then he realised he was hearing footsteps. He had tried to trace them but whatever room he was in they were always in the next one. If he was upstairs they were downstairs, if he was downstairs they were upstairs. If he was in one bedroom they were in the other. He began to sleep badly at nights, laying awake night after night, listening for the footsteps. Some nights they appeared, some nights they didn't. Then one evening as he was in the garden he glanced up to see a face at the upstairs window. Thinking he was the victim of a robbery he paused only to pick up his ceremonial sword he rushed upstairs. There was nobody there. He looked in his wardrobe, in his cupboards, under his bed. There was no one there.

He began to pray. Later that week he purchased a large wooden crucifix that he placed in the second bedroom. Three days later it had disappeared. He bought a second. That too disappeared. He went up to St Mary's church where the vicar allowed him a small bottle of holy water blessed and consecrated by himself. The Captain took the small bottle into the second bedroom. As he opened the stopper and prepared to splash the contents into the four corners of the room a dark shape appeared in the centre of the room. The Captain froze where he was. The shape grew until it formed a large black circle. Then a small white face appeared. As he watched the face seemed to grow as if it were moving forward from a distance. He screamed and the face screamed back. Instinctively he lifted the bottle of holy water and threw its contents into the white face. The thing vanished. Suddenly both the face and the black circle had disappeared. That had been the last straw. He had locked up the house, given the keys to the builders along with a good deposit and precise instructions and left for lodgings in York.

"And sorted out your pension at the same time!" Agnes added as she finished her coffee.

Now he had told his story the man changed, he was more relaxed and less agitated."You do believe me?" he enquired.

Agnes nodded. She believed him. Her truth spell prevented people telling lies. "When will the exorcisms take place?" She asked.

The Captain shook his head. "It won't.

Agnes raised an eyebrow. The Captain continued. "It seems that more proof is needed before the Archbishop will allow such a venture."

Agnes sighed. She had a feeling that she knew the answer to her next question. But she asked it anyway. "I take it you do not intend returning?"

The Captain shook his head. "Once the building has been completed I will place it on sale once again and buy another Scarborough property. I hear Ramshill is an up and coming area."

Agnes nodded. "It is!" she confirmed. She tried to hide her disappointment. The Captain hadn't been able to answer her questions. He had only confirmed what she already knew. Inwardly she felt annoyed at the Archbishop. If he had allowed an exorcism perhaps lives would have been saved. Still hindsight is a wonderful thing.

She invited the Captain to return to the carriage and took him back to his lodgings in Stonegate where they cordially shook hands and where Agnes promised she would visit him when he returned to Scarborough and his new house in Ramsgate.

As the carriage left Stonegate the Captain stood at the entrance to the Old Starr Inn and blinked. He was unsure of what had just happened. He remembered his meeting with the exorcist and his refusal to help. He remembered sitting in a carriage with someone and sitting in a coffee house, but for the life of him he couldn't remember the conversation. It would have prayed on his mind, but by the time he entered the inn he had forgotten the carriage ride and the coffee shop. Uppermost in his mind was the need to find cheaper lodgings.

Despite his meeting with the army paymaster going well he still had to make savings. His army pension wasn't that substantial and the cost of rebuilding was making a hole in his savings.

Chapter Four

Agnes returned to Scarborough and the 21st century where she located the original drawings and compared them with the plans of the house after the Captains alterations. She compared the two. He had widened the staircase making one of the upstairs rooms smaller. The walls had been replaced, the windows widened to let more light in. Downstairs he had moved the kitchen to the rear of the house, they were good improvements, they made sense. She wasn't sure that they were the ideas of the Captain or the builder. She suspected the latter and made a mental note to remember his name, after all, as we've said before, knowing a good, reliable builder is an advantage in whatever century you live in.

She decided to take a walk down Tuthill. Hopefully the press had found some other sensation to aim their questions and cameras at. As she neared the house she noticed that the police guard had been doubled. A blue tent had been erected at the front and rear. Two police vans and a car filled the tiny street. A line of yellow tape closed it off to pedestrians. The way to the top of Customs House Steps was outside the taped off area so she made her way in that direction.

"You alright there love? Going down the stairs?"

She turned to face the police constable who had stepped up to his side of the tape.

"That was my intention!" She replied.

"Just as well, there's nothing to see here!"

The second voice came from the policeman standing nearer to the cottage. She couldn't help herself. "No I don't suppose there is, especially as it's all been on television!"

The second policeman wasn't impressed. "That's as maybe but we've got to keep sightseers away."

"Good job it's not tourist season!" Agnes retorted.

As she spoke she heard the sound of an engine dying and a man covered head to foot in a white suit appeared holding a strimmer.

"They're cutting the garden down then?" Agnes observed nodding in the direction of the man in white.

The constables turned round to look where she had indicated.

"Now who said anything about a...." The first policeman said and stopped when he turned around to discover he was talking to thin air. He looked around."Now where did she go?" He asked the second policeman. He didn't answer. He was too busy fighting off the attentions of a very large and very angry seagull that had taken a liking to the badge on the top of his helmet. When the bird flew off he looked up at his colleague. "What did you say?"

"Nothing!" The first policeman said. He wasn't fond of seagulls at the best of times.

From her position on the chimney pot Agnes looked down at the rear of the house. The grass and most of the plant life had been strimmed to within half an inch of its life. She watched as four men dressed in the white suits were on their hands and knees carrying out a finger tip examination of the garden.

"Good luck with that!" She said to herself. She had scryed the ground from the comfort of her own home and knew the most they would find would be a cannon ball from the English Civil War, a military coat button from the 1800's and the remains of a dead cat buried by its grief stricken owner in 1975.

She pecked and preened her own wing feathers as she thought things through. The police were looking for three missing people last seen in the garden of the little house. No one, except her, had seen anyone actually enter the house and there were no witnesses to the apparition at the window. She asked herself a question, one she should have thought of earlier, why does the face appear and why does it entice people into the upstairs room to disappear them into the blackness. She decided not to ask herself what became of them once they had disappeared, or the nature of the black void, she had enough to think about as it was. Unfortunately, or fortunately depending on one's point of view, Agnes's mind didn't work like that. Another thought struck her. The so-called ghost, the white face at the window didn't haunt the house. It appeared from out of the black void. She remembered what the Captain had told her. He had seen the black shape first and then the white face appeared as if it were travelling towards him, down a tunnel. That meant the white face existed inside the void. It wasn't a ghost, if anything the void was the ghost.

Her chain of thought was broken by a clattering behind her. She turned to see a stone rolling down the roof tiles. She looked into the street. The stone had been thrown by one of the policemen. She watched as it bounced off the gutter and fell into the road.

"Bloody gulls!" She heard him exclaim. She flapped her wings and drifted off on a rising air current that took her over the harbour. She checked the clock on St Mary's Church. It was late morning. She drifted over the pier and found a secluded place to land. The air shimmered and Agnes walked out from between two buildings and headed for the cafe at the end of the pier and had one of their all-day breakfasts.

That evening she spent in her usual seat next to the fireplace in the Three Mariners. Marmaduke had joined her as the builders had stopped working as the light fell. He had nothing to report apart from the fact that the person who seemed to be buying up most of the timber was Andrew Chance, the proprietor of the harbour side chandlery and wheeler dealer extraordinaire. She sighed. The man had a nose for spotting a profit. No cargo came or went though Scarborough's Harbour without him knowing about it, legal or illegal. No doubt he had a buyer already lined up. She made a mental note to have a word with him.

Eavesdropping on bar room conversations she

realised that most of the talk seemed to be about the building work in the house on Tuthill.

"Won't make a ha'pence or difference!" A voice next to her proclaimed.

She turned and looked at Old Sam who was tapping out the ash from his clay pipe. She watched as, once he knew he had her attention, he replaced the pipe into his mouth and sucked noisily. It was a noise like a drain emptying, only not as savoury. She rummaged in her pocket and pulled out a small plug of tobacco that she held between her thumb and forefinger.

"Now why won't the rebuilding make any difference?"

Old Sam looked at the small brown lump and then looked up at Agnes.

"Cos the place was haunted afore the house was built!"

Agnes sighed. What he was saying didn't make any sense. Then she realised he had used the word "place".

"You mean the site was haunted before the house

was built?" she asked.

Sam looked at her. "That's what I said!"

She passed him the tobacco and watched as he cut and twisted it with a small pocket knife before cramming it into the bowl of his pipe.

"What was there before?" She asked.

Old Sam struck a match, placed it on the bowl and sucked and spluttered and sucked until he exhaled a huge cloud of smoke. He took the pipe out of his mouth and peered into the bowl.

"Eh missus, how old do you think I am? Yon house were built over seventy years ago."

She held his gaze. "And just how old are you Sam? Oh and before you say anything remember, I've know you for a lot of years!"

Sam shifted and looked down at his feet. "Seventy five next August!"

Agnes waved her hand to disperse the cloud of smoke that hung between them. "In which case...."

Old Sam cut her off. "In which case you should

remember yourself." Then he gave his pipe another suck and sent another plume of smoke between them.

Agnes took a sip of her brandy and thought back. She had moved into her house in 1712 when she had inherited it from an unfortunate sea captain who had a very dubious career. She had done him a great favour and in return he had left her his house in his will. She thought once more and dredged her memory. As far as she could remember the Tuthill house had already been built when she moved in, and before that? Well Agnes never liked to think of her times before that. Back then she was a different person in a different world. A world she had no memory of. The only thing Agnes knew about her past was that she had always been a witch and always three hundred years old. To be truthful she wasn't even sure that Agnes was her real name.
She gave a little shake of her head and drained her glass. It was no good thinking like that. She turned back to Sam.

"Humour me, what was there before the house?" As she spoke she gave him one of her special looks.

He blinked "Pig sties" he replied.

It wasn't the answer Agnes expected. Sam continued. "They were made out of the ruins of the old cottages that stood there since ancient times!"

Agnes looked down at her glass. It had been refilled. She looked across to where Baccy Lad was walking back to the bar. She smiled as she noticed how much he had benefitted from his recent adventure with her. The tan and pierced ears suited him. She raised her glass in his direction and took a sip.

She turned her attention back to Sam "I don't suppose there were any stories about strange things happening back then?"

"Pigs never mentioned anything!" he replied.

Agnes was tempted to ask for the tobacco back. The only thing that stopped her was the realisation that whatever it was pre-dated the house. Perhaps it even pre-dated the pig sties. Perhaps the answer lay in the ancient times as Old Sam had suggested.

"There were some rumours though!" he added.

Some rumours! She sat back and looked into the fireplace. Next to her Old Sam had fallen into a
68

silence, even his pipe had stopped it's gurgling. He too had drifted off into private thoughts, of years earlier when he was a young lad. When he'd lean over the wall and watch the pigs snuffling and grunting in the churned up mud of their small enclosure. He remembered it was where he ran to cry when the news came that his father had been lost at sea. It was then his life changed. Within months he was a cabin boy on a coal ship travelling between Newcastle and London. It was no good him protesting. It was no good him wanting to be a pig farmer. It was just the way it was. He raised his hand and wiped a grubby sleeve at a watering eye. Agnes chose not to notice.

Chapter Five

The following morning Agnes was sat at her computer in her 21st century living room. She searched web site after web site, eventually settling on the site of the Scarborough Archaeological Society. That was illuminating. There were articles about all periods of Scarborough's history. She was tempted to read one on medieval witchcraft, but decided it wouldn't be very flattering. She had no stomach to read of the cruel treatments and punishments meted out to the elderly ladies that had the temerity to treat aches and pains with herbs and common sense, and who owned cats.

Eventually she found what she had been looking for. The story of the Old Town. She skim read a lot, taking in a fact here, ignoring something there. After an hour she had an outline. The headland and the site of the Castle dated back to the Iron Age and the Romans. The town settlement was founded by Vikings and destroyed by them. She knew all about that having witnessed the invasion for herself. She smiled as she remembered a particular past adventure and knew that history wasn't always correct. Then everything went quiet until a King named Stephen made a Norman Knight, the
70

Earl of York. William de Gros was an ambitious man and in a period of England's history when Barons and Lords fought to capture and keep what they could, he grabbed Scarborough and built a castle on the headland. During its construction hamlets and shacks sprang up below its walls housing tradesmen, servants, fisher folk, people who discovered they could scratch a living by supplying the Castle and its inhabitants with good, locally sourced produce. Now she had a date. It was a long time back, but it was a date. Now she had a date she had somewhere, something to fix her concentration on. All she had to do was to follow the time line of the building from its construction to it becoming a pig sty. Just a matter of six hundred years or so.

She sighed when she realised she had no idea of what she was looking for, but she filled her scrying bowl all the same. She cast her usual scrying spell and added some special ingredients. Scrying through time was a bit more complicated and called for different herbs and a lot more effort. She rolled up her sleeves and began the process, starting at the beginning, back to the days of William le Gros.

At first she didn't recognise the Headland. Erosion and time had changed it. She moved her hand and

71

the vision changed to an overhead view of the land that would become Tuthill. Just like Google Earth she thought, and then wondered if she could bring a case of copyright or plagiarism at the very least. She shook her head and smiled. English law didn't take witchcraft into consideration when it came to copyright law, or any other law for that matter, unless it involved burning at the stake.

Below her time passed. The 12th century became the 13th. Buildings rose and were pulled down and replaced. She moved her hands, the images stopped and the water became cloudy. This was getting her nowhere, and not very fast. She flicked her fingers and the computer shut down. She descended the stairs into the cellar and re-emerged in the 18th century.

It was early evening when she reached Tuthill. At first she thought the house was deserted, then she saw some movement in the front downstairs window. She stopped to look. She wasn't surprised that the slight noise behind her. She turned to find Marmaduke had melted out of the shadows.

"It's Andrew. He's in there checking on the timbers!" He whispered in her ear.

She sighed. "Let's see shall we!"

Without hesitation she strode up the little path and straight into the entrance. She didn't have to bother turning a door knob or opening the front door. The door wasn't there. It was propped up inside the front room as Andrew measured it.

"I take it you're making a good profit out of all this timber!" She said.

Unfazed Andrew continued with his measuring. "A fair profit, and its all above board!"

Agnes raised an eyebrow. "If I thought for one minute that was an intentional pun!"

Andrew stood up with a smile on his face. "It was rather good don't you think?"

Agnes just shook her head and looked across at the staircase. It was still standing.

"I haven't touched the stairs." Andrew said.

"You've not found a customer for them yet you mean!" She replied.

"I need to get upstairs. I've someone interested in the floorboards."

Agnes walked to the bottom of the stairs. "Come on then. There's no time like the present."

She took a step and then stopped. There was a noise upstairs. She turned back to Andrew. "Any of your lads up there?"

Andrew shook his head and looked at the ceiling above him. Agnes turned to Marmaduke who was standing at the doorway. He gave a nod and silently entered the building. As he passed Agnes he gave a bound and the air around him shimmered. A shape half man half large cat appeared on the top step. A door upstairs slammed shut.

Andrew wasn't quite sure what happened next. There was a flash of light. He blinked. When he opened his eyes Agnes wasn't there anymore. He heard more noise above him and without thinking ran upstairs. When he reached the top he saw the door to the second bedroom had been ripped off its hinges and lay in various pieces on the floor of the room. He peered inside. It was black, pitch black. Suddenly something grabbed him by the arms and dragged him to one side. He turned to see Marmaduke's hand on his arm. In front of him the darkness seemed to be getting bigger. Then there was another flash and he heard Agnes's voice shout one word.

"Jump!"

He jumped. Then he fell. It seemed he was falling down a deep well. Then a feint light began to glow. He turned. Marmaduke was falling next to him. The glow brightened and the air around him popped. He had stopped falling. He opened his eyes to find himself inside a large bubble. Marmaduke was standing next to him. They looked at each other.

"Where's Agnes?" Andrew asked when he found his voice.

Marmaduke looked around him. "I think she might be the bubble!" he said.

It was too much for Andrew. "I need to sit down before I feint!" He said and squatted down on his haunches. Then he tested the strength of the bubble and stretched his legs out in front of him.

Marmaduke squatted down next to him. "Are we still falling?" He asked after a few minutes.

Marmaduke shook his head. "I've no idea!"

Andrew looked around him. "I take it you've no idea of what's happening either?"

Marmaduke looked down and shook his head. "I went upstairs. Someone slammed a door in my face. I smashed it open. In front of me was a large black shape. It was growing. Then a face came out of it. Before I could do anything there was a flash and Agnes appeared in front of me and shouted "jump". Then you appeared. I grabbed you and we fell into the darkness."

"I didn't fall. It swallowed me!" Andrew recalled.

Before Marmaduke could reply it suddenly wasn't dark anymore. There was a bump and they both fell over. When they stood up they were standing on firm ground. The bubble had disappeared. The air shimmered and Agnes was standing in front of them. She glanced at their faces, and then looked around. Then she looked back at her companions and brushed down the front of her skirts. "Well that was interesting. Unexpected I'll grant you, but interesting!"

Andrew looked around. "Where are we?"

Agnes looked around. The landscape was sparse,

everything seemed to be shades of grey. In the distance she could make out small hills and rocky outcrops. It appeared to her that they were in the middle of a desert.

Marmaduke looked up into the black sky. "There's no stars!"

Agnes twitched her fingers and a small cloud of dust rose some feet in front of her. She clicked her fingers and small sparks appeared. She winked at Andrew and he sneezed.

"Well my tricks seem intact!" She remarked.

"Where are we?" Andrew repeated.

Agnes looked at him. "I won't say I've no idea. I've lots of ideas, but right here, right now, I'm not too sure!"

Andrew let out a sound that was a cross between a sigh, a groan and a short sob.

Whilst Agnes had been testing her powers and talking to Andrew Marmaduke had been staring out over the surroundings. His pupils had narrowed and he was looking at the landscape through his cats eyes. He felt his whiskers twitch. He could sense something. His eyes narrowed. Something had just moved among the distant rocks. Before anyone realised what was happening he changed into his large cat form and bounded across the sand and the rocks until he came to the outcrop. There was a blur of movement and suddenly Marmaduke wasn't alone. Back in his human form he found he was holding the figure of a small man dressed in a pair of much worn leggings and a battered leather tunic held around his waist by a broad belt that once held a dagger. The man's face was grey and lined. His eyes were wide and his mouth opened and closed in silence as he looked down at his own dagger that was being held at his throat. He tried to swallow but stopped when he realised his Adam's apple was resting on the tip of his blade. He stopped swallowing. Marmaduke snarled and the man gave a shiver.

"Don't bat an eyelid!" Marmaduke said and withdrew the dagger slightly. There was another blur and the man found himself flat on his back with his attacker standing over him.

"Who are you?" Marmaduke asked.

The man laid where he was as one of his hands explored his own throat. He pulled it back to see if there was any blood on his fingers. There wasn't.

He looked up.

"I should be asking you that!" he replied.

"Well we asked first!" The man turned around to see Agnes standing behind him. Another figure stood next to her. The man knew he stood no chance against the three of them.

"Why were you watching us?" Agnes asked.

"I wondered who you are. I don't see many others around here." The man said struggling to raise himself on one arm.

Agnes was puzzled. "When did you last see anyone?" she asked.

The man looked confused. "Some time ago. Not far away, not near!"

"How many days ago?" Andrew asked thinking that after Marmaduke's attack the man might be concussed.

The man turned to Andrew. "Days? Were there days?" he cocked his head as if trying to remember.

Agnes looked down at the man and gently let her mind probe his memory, just slightly, just enough for her to realise that the man only had a vague concept of the word. Then a penny dropped. Wherever they were didn't have a night or day. Then a second penny followed the first. If the place had no day or night, did any time actually pass?

"How long have you been here?" She asked. The man just stared back at her. He didn't know. She turned to Andrew. "The man has no concept of time!"

Despite being a merchant and the importer of certain goods Andrew had spent some time at sea. He looked up at the dense blackness of the starless sky. "If there's no stars surely there can be no directions. There is no north and no south, or if there is there's no way of telling which is which!"

Marmaduke stroked his whiskers. "There's no wind. The air is still. I wonder if that means there's no weather?"

Agnes stared at the little man. "Where do we go from here?" The man looked up and pointed into the distance. "Take us!" she said.

Before the man could react Agnes moved her finger and the man found himself standing up. Without a second glance he suddenly set off walking. The three of them followed him.
The man led them across a flat plain, towards another rocky outcrop before veering slightly to his left.

"If you are thinking of leading us around in circles I would think again." Agnes warned him. The man reverted to his original line.

Eventually they made out a shape on the horizon. Within a few steps it had come nearer. It was the shape of a house. With each step they took the house grew larger, as if the house was coming to meet them. Then they found themselves standing at the door of a large, three story house built in a style that could be only described as Gothic meets American Wild West. It was the same grey colour as the surrounding landscape. Its windows were black, no light showed from them. The man stopped at the door and turned to Agnes.

"I can go no further!"

Marmaduke raised the dagger. Agnes held up her hand. "No he's right. It's not that he won't, he can't. Something will not allow him through the

81

door. She turned to the little man. "Wait!" Then she stepped forward. The door opened as she approached and the three of them entered the building.

They took a few steps into a large square hall. Doors led to the right and the left. In front of them a staircase led to upper floors. The first thing Agnes noticed was that there was no colour. Everything was grey. Suddenly a white shape flew at them from down the staircase. They stood their ground as the apparition flew in their faces. A mouth appeared and let out a silent scream. Just as it seemed it would crash into them it shot upwards and disappeared into the ceiling above their heads. Marmaduke pulled out his sword and Andrew pulled a pistol from inside his jacket as a second white shape shot through the opposite wall and headed towards them. Marmaduke slashed at it but the blade just passed through it as if it were smoke.

"Ghosts!" Andrew cried, lifting his arm to protect his face.

Agnes clicked her fingers and attuned her senses. Whatever was happening wasn't any type of magic she'd ever come across. She let her senses reach out, creeping through the house like tentacles of ivy. She felt some sort of vibration. She tried to work out what it was. It was neither good nor bad. It wasn't magic, but it wasn't of her material world.

She was still sensing when a movement caught her eye. She turned to see a figure appear to walk out of the wall opposite her. She blinked. It was the figure of an Elizabethan gentleman, complete with tights and a ruff around its neck. However the thing that they noticed first of all was that it was carrying its head under its arm. Agnes did a double take. This was a thing of cheap theatrical tricks, the ghost that music hall jokes were made from. It was a cliché. She watched as the figure ignored the three people in the hall and continued walking through the opposite wall and presumably outside the building.

"We're in a haunted house!" Andrew exclaimed.

Agnes looked across at him. "It seems that way!" Then she remembered something someone had recently said. Perhaps ghosts are just a different sort of magic. Well if it was, it was a sort of magic she had no knowledge of.
Suddenly what little light there was began to dim and flash, giving the effect of a broken strobe light. She clicked her finger and an orb of soft glowing light appeared and illuminated the hallway. Agnes

noticed that paintings hung on the walls and up, along the side of the staircase. Sculptures stood on plinths, all of them in shades of grey. It was as if they had been transported into a black and white movie where someone had kidnapped the white. Forget the fifty shades of grey, Agnes realised she was in a world of fifty thousand shades of grey. She turned to Marmaduke noticed that his ginger beard was turning a shade greyer. The colour of his coat and jacket was fading. She turned to Andrew. His colourful waistcoat wasn't as colourful. She glanced down at her own skirts. It looked as if she had put them through a hot wash, the colours had run and they were turning grey.

"I think we need to get out of here!" She said quietly.

Marmaduke turned towards the door they had entered through. He stopped and blinked. It wasn't there. He turned to Agnes.

"Keep walking, it's just an illusion!" Agnes remarked.
Marmaduke continued walking until he walked straight into a wall where the door had been. It hurt. He held his nose as he turned back to Agnes.

"There again, perhaps it isn't!" She said.

She put a hand out in front of her and wriggled her fingers. Marmaduke and Andrew watched as Agnes closed her eyes.

"Keep walking forward, then take one step to the left, turn right and walk forward again!"

They followed her instructions and found themselves outside the house.

"Right!" she said, "Let's sit down and have a think about this." She clicked her fingers and three very comfortable armchairs appeared. They say down.

"What about him?" Marmaduke asked nodding towards the small man who was still standing by the front door of the house.

"Leave him where he is for the moment!" Agnes replied.

Andrew gave a strained laugh. Agnes and Marmaduke turned to him. "It just struck me as funny. The man has no notion of time. He could stand there for a moment, an hour, a day, or until the end of time and it would make no difference."

Agnes blinked. "Repeat that!" She said.

Andrew stopped laughing. "It wasn't that funny!"

"The bit you said it would make no difference if he stood a day or a week!"

"Till the end of time!" Marmaduke added and looked around at the flat barren landscape and black sky.

"That's the bit!" Agnes said.

Realising what was being suggested Andrew looked around him. "You mean we're at the end of time?" He asked quietly.

They all fell silent as they thought the idea over, then Andrew pointed towards the house. "If this is the end of time what's a haunted house doing here?"

Agnes scratched her head. "That Andrew is a very good question!" She began to rummage in her pocket and pulled out her scrying bowl. She placed it on her knee and filled it with water from a small flask that seemed to appear from nowhere. A handful of herbs and spices followed. Then she passed her hand over it and looked down. She was looking at the hallway of the house in front of them. She moved her vision and allowed it to move from room to room. Whenever she moved she saw the same thing, neatly laid out rooms dressed with Georgian furniture, chairs, cabinets, carpets and large pictures on the walls. It appeared to be a typical Georgian Mansion apart from the fact that everything was a shade of grey. Inside a room lined with books that she assumed was a library she saw movement. She held the image and watched a figure of a tall elegant grey lady walk across the room and walk through the wall opposite into the hallway. She moved her vision to the hall. There was no one there.

She moved upstairs and passed from room to room pausing to look at the Elizabethan gentleman who was pacing up and down in a corridor still holding his head under his arm. A white face loomed into view. It turned and looked straight at Agnes. Instinctively she pulled her hand back and flicked a spell at the bowl of water. The shape of the screaming face emerged from the water and suddenly stopped as it seemed to hit something invisible. It opened its mouth wider, turned and vanished back into the water.

Agnes looked up at her companions. Marmaduke was standing with a pistol in one hand and a dagger in the other. Andrew was standing with a half drawn pistol in his hand, his mouth wide open.

I wonder what would have happened if it got loose!" Agnes pondered. The she noticed. "Your colour's coming back! It must be something to do with being outside the house!"

Andrew and Marmaduke exchanged looks but before they could make any comment Agnes spoke once again. "You two stay here whilst I have a look around."

Before either of them could comment the air around her blurred and was filled with a great deal of fluttering and flapping. A great bird appeared and launched itself into the black sky. Marmaduke and Andrew watched as it beat its wings and ascended into the air where it was lost in the darkness.

"What by all the seas was that?" Andrew gasped. Marmaduke looked at the sky. "I think it was a vulture!" he replied.

Once she was airborne Agnes looked down at the landscape spread below her. To say it was bleak was to use the word bleak in its most extreme form. It was a deserted desert, featureless, empty. She rose higher and sent out her feelings. There was something, an undulation some distance away from the house. She gave a few beats of her wings and glided over it. She was passing over some piles of stone. Her interest aroused she circled over it and then landed.

The air shimmered and Agnes appeared standing at the side of a line of rubble. She bent down. It was the remains of a wall. She realised that she was standing in the ruins of a building that had once stood on the site. She walked the length of the wall, examining where it intersected with other traces of walls. Agnes clicked her fingers and the footprint of the building began to glow. It appeared that once it had been a large building, or a complex of smaller individual buildings. She closed her eyes and moved her hands. A vision rose in her mind. She could see a large domed building with two wings complete with towers. Light bounced from the gold that covered the dome and the tops of the towers. The building was surrounded by a neat garden laid out in a variety of shapes, surrounded by palm trees. It looked very much like the building used to be a palace. She shook her head and the vision disappeared. She opened her eyes and gazed out over the barren landscape once again.

A feint noise caught her attention and noticed a small cloud of dust appear on the horizon. She remained where she was until the cloud got nearer. She concentrated and looked through the dust. She blinked as she took in the sight. It was a rather large man dressed in a tweed suite, complete with a pair of plus four trousers and wearing a deerstalker hat. His face was obscured by a pair of large goggles. His hands were covered by a large pair of leather gauntlets, gripping the steering wheel of a very early vintage car, they type of which was usually seen in the London to Brighton vintage rally. It was an open topped four seater that moved along on four large spoked wheels and had a thick leather belt strapped around its long bonnet at the end of which were two headlamps. What made it stand out even more was that it was painted bright yellow.

It was the first colour Agnes had seen since she had arrived wherever she was. At first glance she thought she was seeing the famous Chitty Chitty Bang Bang and that any minute it would sprout wings and fly away.

For reasons beyond her understanding she found herself waving. The driver saw her and turned the wheel slightly to drive towards her. As he approached he seemed to be waving his hand at her in a gesture that clearly said "get out of the way!"

"No time, no time!" The man shouted.

"We'll see about that!" Agnes said to herself as she flicked a finger. The car engine gave a couple of splutters and died, just as it came to a stop next to her. The driver looked her up and down, looked back at his dashboard and pulled a lever. Nothing happened. He jumped down from the driving seat, pulled out a crank shaft and ran to the front of the car where he inserted the shaft and began turning it. He tried again and again, but nothing happened. Finally he let out a whoop of frustration and kicked the front of the radiator.

"I'm not sure kicking it will start it up again!" Agnes observed.

The man continued staring at the front of the vehicle. "She! It's a she, not an it!"

"Even more reason not to kick it!" Agnes replied.

The man turned towards her as if seeing her for the first time. "Who the devil are you?" As he spoke he lifted the goggles revealing a youngish face with blond eyebrows and blues eyes.
"Just a traveller like yourself." Agnes replied.

The man looked confused. "Travelling? Yes I'm travelling!"

"May I enquire as to where you've come from and where you're going?"

The man looked at her. She gave him one of those looks. He looked back in the direction from where he had just come. He lifted an arm and pointed. "From there!" he said and then turned to where he had been heading and pointed once more. "To there!"

Agnes nodded. "How long have you been driving?"

The man thought for a few seconds. It was obvious that the question puzzled him. To confirm his puzzlement he lifted the front of his deerstalker and scratched the front of his head.

"I've always driven!" he said eventually.

Agnes looked at the car and then back to the man then back to the car again. "I suppose you have." She paused. "Why did you shout the words "no time"?"

The man remained looking puzzled. "Did I?"

Agnes nodded. The man thought for a few seconds before answering her very slowly, thinking before each sentence. "Either I'm late or there is no time. If there is no time, I can't be late. However if I am late, it must mean there is time and if there is time I must be on my way before time runs out, or I'll be late."

Agnes thought she understood what the man was saying. She changed the subject. "That's a very nice car you have there."

The man turned and admired his machine. Forgetting it had let him down he patted the bonnet. "Timeless." He said.

"In which case as your car is timeless, you can't be late, and if you can't be late can I trouble you for a lift over in that direction?" She pointed to where she had left Marmaduke and Andrew.

The man walked to the passenger side and opened the door. "I would be delighted, so pleasant to have some company. I'm sure the old girl would like the novelty of carrying a passenger."

Agnes climbed into the passenger seat and settled down as the driver returned to the crankshaft. As
93

he turned the handle Agnes moved her finger and the engine fired up and throbbed softly as the driver jumped aboard.

It seemed that they arrived the moment they set off. As the car drew to a halt outside the haunted house the driver looked around and then down at the controls and patted the dashboard. "Well done old girl." He said.

Next to him Agnes pondered on the strange fact that here, wherever here was, where time didn't exist, how was it possible for her to manage to cast a spell to make the car go faster? After a few seconds she decided she didn't need to know. It just worked. Agnes was a great believer in the old saying that "If it ain't broke, don't fix it!"

When the dust settled and he wiped the dust from his eyes Andrew looked at this strange machine that had appeared out of a minor dust storm. "What in the world is that?" He asked.

Agnes began climbing out of the passenger seat. "It's called a motor car. It will replace horses in years to come. Everyone will have one and on every public holiday people will sit in them end to end, not moving, hoping that they will get somewhere before its time for them to go back."

Andrew looked confused.

"Think of it as a mechanical horse" She added brushing the dust from her skirts.

"Who's the driver and what's that on his head?" Marmaduke asked.

"He seems to spend his time driving from nowhere to nowhere else, and the thing on his head is a hat called a deerstalker. It has flaps to keep your ears warm."

Marmaduke didn't seem impressed. Agnes turned to the driver "Do you have a name?"

The man stopped brushing the dust from his tweeds and looked to the horizon. "Name? Must have had a name once. Damned if I remember it now." He turned back to Agnes. "Call me George." He said.

Agnes cocked her head. "Is that your name?" The driver shook his head. "No idea but I've always liked the name George."

"I don't suppose you know where we are?" Andrew asked.

George turned towards him. "We're here!" He answered.

Andrew shook his head. "But where is here?"

George looked at him. "Not over there!"

Andrew sighed. Agnes indicated at the house. "What do you know about the haunted house?" George looked it up and down. "Never seen it before!" he remarked.

She pointed at the little man still standing by the door. "What about him?"

George walked over to him and peered at him before turning back to Agnes. "He's a Wally."

Agnes did a double take. All sorts of thoughts suddenly rose and fell in her mind. Ignoring her own creativity she simply asked, "What's a Wally?"

George shrugged. "Little fellows, just like him. They live out there in the wilderness. Come across them from time to time."
"Why are they called Wally?" She asked.

"Because I'm always finding them!" George replied with a straight face.

Agnes looked around to see if anyone was laughing. No one was. She looked closely at George and was tempted to use a truth spell but didn't. She decided to change tack. "Just how many people are out there?"

George paused for a while and scratched his head. "I don't really know. I've never counted them." Agnes cocked her eyebrow. George puzzled her, it wasn't that he wasn't very bright, he was. It was as if he had no knowledge of time or place. He was happy in his own little world, which was driving his car. Agnes wondered if the car ever ran out of petrol and decided not to ask, instead she gave him another of her looks. "Do you remember a time before driving?"

George looked straight at her. "Can't say I can." He replied.

Agnes knew he was telling the truth. Her magic told her so. It also told her that somewhere deep inside him, a feint memory lurked, but it was impossible to reach. Whoever he was, or had been, was lost. She glanced at the landscape surrounding them. He wasn't the only one. They were all lost.

She looked back at the haunted house. She was convinced it held some sort of clue. Then she had a think, there was no way of avoiding it. She turned to Marmaduke and Andrew. "We're going back inside!"

The colour drained from Andrews face. Agnes looked at him. "You're not afraid of ghosts are you?"

Andrew looked back. "Yes!"

"Well this time we're going inside better prepared!" She replied and began rummaging around in her pocket. After she had pulled out a ball of string, a sprig of heather and a small, evil smelling little leather bag she eventually found what she was looking for, a small glass crystal ball. She held it up and peered into it, then gave it a rub with her sleeve, breathed on it and gave it another polish. A light deep inside it flickered and began to glow.

"Right, in we go!" She said.

Before the three of them took a step forward George gave a little cough. They turned to him. "I say chaps, you don't mind if I tag along?"

Agnes nodded and looked across to the Wally. He shook his head.

Agnes opened the door. It wasn't locked and gave a satisfying creak as it swung open and the four of them stepped inside the hallway.

As soon as the door closed behind them a white face screamed out of nearby wall covering the space between them in just enough time to allow Agnes to click her finger. There was a slight plop and the face disappeared. She looked down at the orb. A small white blob was floating around in the faint light. She smiled and held the orb above her head. From nowhere dozens of screaming faces swept down at them only to disappear inside the orb.

"What about the chap with no head?" George asked.

Agnes turned towards him. "How do you know about him?"

George pointed to the top of the stairs. "He was standing up there!"

Agnes pulled herself upright and marched towards the staircase. "Follow me!" She ordered. No one was inclined to argue. George was directly behind her with Andrew behind him. Marmaduke brought up the rear with a drawn sword in one hand and a pistol in the other. He was open minded about ghosts but still believed in not taking any chances. If there was anything, or anyone who was thinking of attacking he was ready, willing and certainly more than able.

As Agnes arrived to the top of the stairs she lifted the orb above her head and moved her fingers. Half a dozen more screaming white faces disappeared inside, followed by a rather started lady dressed in grey. She held onto her bonnet as she disappeared inside the orb.

"Do you really think you can fool me with that cheap trick!" A voice behind her suddenly said.

Agnes turned to come face to face with the headless ghost. Well she would have been face to face if its head had been on the top of its shoulders, where you expect a head to be. She blinked as she realised she was looking at the opposite wall.

"Down here!" The voice said.

Agnes looked down at the head neatly tucked underneath the man's arm.

"I do apologise!" She said.

"Easy mistake to make!" The man remarked.

Despite it being disconcerting to talk to an unattached head Agnes continued. "I'll have you know it took a lot of practise to learn that particular trick!" She said.

The head gave a snort. "Call that a trick! I have better ones up my sleeve." It added and then disappeared.

Agnes looked up. The head was where is should be. Back on top of the man's shoulders. "So I see, so why won't my trick work on you?"

Before the man could answer Agnes answered for him. "Because you're not a ghost!"
The man laughed. Agnes ignored him. "You're not even a man are you?"

The man stopped laughing. Agnes looked closely at him "Of course that poses another question. If you're not a man, just what are you?"

The man tried a look of pretend mortification. "Madam, I must assure you. I am the ghost of one
101

Piers Gaveston, First Earl of Cornwall and once proud owner of Scarborough Castle."

Agnes gave a tut and moved her hand and fingers. The man froze, his mouth half open, fixed in his protestations. She gave him one of her special looks. "Right, you're not a ghost, certainly not of Piers Gaveston. Your dress is wrong. Ruffs didn't arrive until Elizabethan times and you were born in the 13th century. So...." she paused to gather her thoughts. "You have knowledge of the world outside, you know of Scarborough Castle and its history, so your knowledge extends beyond this place."

She moved nearer to the frozen man. "You're the Gatekeeper aren't you?"

As she spoke she clicked her fingers and her spell was broken. The man smiled and gave a little bow. "Congratulations lady, you are most perceptive." As he spoke the air around him shimmered and the Elizabethan gentleman faded away to be replaced by a taller figure in a grey cloak and a cowl pulled over his head, Agnes peered into the cowl. A long grey face peered back at her, even his hair and pupils of his eyes were grey.

Throughout the conversation the three others had remained at the top of the staircase. Marmaduke, weapons still in hand, kept glancing to his right and left. Andrew kept looking down the staircase and glancing at the hallway below. George just stared open mouthed at the apparition in front of him.

Agnes placed her hands together as if in prayer and gave a little bow in return. "Greetings Gatekeeper. I have heard of your kind, but never met one of your like."

His voice came from out of the cowl. "No there has been no reason for our paths to cross. Indeed I am puzzled as to why they cross here and now."

Agnes looked around her before turning back to the grey figure. "Gatekeeper. For the sake of my back, and my companions patience, may I suggest we retire to a more suitable position. I have a feeling we have a long conversation ahead and I'd really like to sit down."

The Gatekeeper turned. "Follow!" he said.

He led them away from the staircase and towards a door at the rear of the landing. As he approached, it opened revealing a dark wood panelled room inset with bookshelves filled with thousands of

103

leather bound volumes. At the far end of the room, sat inside a bay window, was a large, ornate desk. The figure indicated a circle of four armchairs that faced towards it. As they took their seats Marmaduke remained standing and moved behind the chair Agnes has chosen. The grey man looked up from behind his desk. "You can sit cat-man. She needs no protection here!"

Marmaduke looked uneasy, Agnes turned and nodded towards the empty chair. He sat down but placed the pistol across his knees. Agnes turned back to the man behind his desk. "Why here, why now? Those are very good questions, but first it would prove useful to discuss where is here?"

The Gatekeeper shrugged. "Surely you know!" Agnes nodded. "I have my thoughts, but for the sake of my companions an explanation would be useful."

The Gatekeeper looked across the others. "I am the Gatekeeper. You are on the opposite side of the gate!"

Andrew let out a little start and jumped to his feet. "You say...oh no! You're death. You're saying we're dead and we're in the land of the dead!" he sat back, sighed and began to fan himself.

Marmaduke raised his eyebrow. He certainly didn't feel dead. The Gatekeeper shook his head. "In this place there is no death!"

Agnes leant forward. I don't suppose you've heard of a certain Captain George Deaconsfield by any chance?"

The Gatekeeper sat back in his chair and thought for a few seconds. "Ah the religious one. I remember him. He dismantled his house you know. Sold off all the timber!"

Andrew looked up and the Gatekeeper smiled. "I know of you Andrew Chance. I will watch the destination of the timbers you sell!"

Agnes clicked her tongue. "So Andrew has yet to sell his reclaimed timber?"
The Gatekeeper smiled. "As you well know he was sizing up the timber when the unfortunate series of events occurred to being you here, but as you ask, yes he is buying the timber, he has also sold the timber and the house has also been sold."

The three men in the room looked puzzled. Agnes gave a nod. "So what you are saying is that all time is happening consecutively?"
105

The Gatekeeper sighed and shook his head. "What I am saying is there is no time. Therefore all time is now."

Agnes closed her eyes and opened them again. She was beginning to get a headache. She shuffled herself upright and leant slightly forward, always a dangerous sign. "Do you know I don't really care about this time thing. Whatever is happening was happening before we arrived and will continue after we've gone, which incidentally is what I intend to concentrate my efforts on."

She moved slightly more forward. The Gatekeeper noticed and moved slightly back in his chair. Marmaduke noticed the movement and realised that Agnes had taken charge of the situation. She continued speaking. "And you are going to help me. Now stop pontificating. What's going on?"

The Gatekeeper sighed and reached down to pull a drawer out of the desk. There was a clink and he placed a bottle of brandy in front of him. He repeated the motion, this time bringing up five glasses. He poured the drinks and slid the glasses across the desk. As everyone leant forward to take their drinks the Gatekeeper continued.

"This is a timeless place. A crossroads as it were. It has gateways. One of those has gone rogue."

"Gateways to where?" Andrew asked.

The Gatekeeper asked him. "Gateways from here to there."

"From one world to another, or should I say, from one reality to another." Agnes explained.

The Gatekeeper looked at her. "Very nicely put!"

"What do you mean rogue?" Marmaduke asked.

The Gatekeeper looked at him. "I mean the thing is moving around. It's all over the place, travelling through time, dragging people and things into it and dropping them, well who knows where. Some, like George there, end up here." At the sound of his name George simply raised his glass in a slight toast.

"You said things." Agnes said.

The Gatekeeper spread his arms. "How do you think this haunted house got here? It's not meant to be here at all."

"Where is it meant to be?" Andrew asked.

The Gatekeeper gave a slight shrug. "Who knows?"

"Why did you pretend to be a ghost?" Agnes asked.

The Gatekeeper smiled. "It amused me!"

"So how do you know about Scarborough?" Andrew asked.

"Good question!" Agnes observed.

"It is a place where the rogue gateway keeps returning to. For some reason it seems drawn there."

"Where else does it go?" Agnes asked.

The Gatekeeper shook his head. "If I could answer you that I could find out where this house came from. By the way, just what did you do with the ghosts. I tried everything I could to get rid of them."

Agnes tapped her pocket. "I've put them away for another day." She saw the look of surprise on the
108

Gatekeepers face. "Oh don't worry. I'll put them back. I'll release them when the time is right. They belong here."

With that she produced the globe and carefully placed it on the desk. Inside the white faces could be seen moving around. One came up to the glass and gave a silent scream.

"Annoying things!" The Gatekeeper observed. "Harmless of course."

"How did the ghosts get out of this house and into the Gateways?" Agnes asked.

The Gatekeeper looked at her, not understanding her meaning.

"It was the faces that attracted the people to enter the gateway." She explained.

The Gatekeeper showed genuine shock. "I had not associated the two." He said and paused to give the matter some thought.

As he fell silent Andrew looked across at Agnes. "Would you humour me, but can I just run through a couple of things, just for my own piece of mind?"

Agnes hid a smiled as she nodded. Andrew continued. "We are somewhere where time doesn't exist, in a sort of crossroads where gateways exist allowing things to pass from... wherever to wherever. I don't really want to think about that. What I do want to think about is, and correct me if I'm wrong, the only way we can get back is to find one of these gateways, the one that's gone missing, and go back through it?"

He stopped to take a breath. Agnes nodded. "That's about the head and tail of it." She replied.

George looked from one face to another. "I fell into a hole!" He said. "The odd thing about it was that it wasn't in the ground. It just appeared standing in the middle of the road. Couldn't stop in time. I seemed to be falling forever."

"His memory is returning!" Marmaduke observed. Agnes nodded.

"Can you remember where and when you fell into the hole?" She asked.

George closed his eyes and thought hard. "Banbury to Oxford Road. It was late morning."

110

"I meant the year." Agnes said.

George looked at her. "This year of course. 1910!"

"His 1910, he means." The Gatekeeper remarked with his eyes closed.

"He's from the future!"Andrew remarked.

The Gatekeeper re-opened his eyes. "You're from his past. It's all the same. We're all just here."

Before anyone could work out what he meant Marmaduke asked a question. "What about the Wallys?"

The Gatekeeper scratched his head. "From what I remember they've always been here. At one point I thought they were born here, but there again, I've never seen a young one, or an old one for that matter."

The group fell silent again.

"You said the gateway returns to the Scarborough house. Where does it return to, I mean where is it when it's here?"

111

The Gatekeeper looked at Agnes. "The rest of the gateways are in fixed positions across the landscape. The rogue one appears and disappears in random places."

"Does it ever reappear where it should be?" Andrew asked.

The Gatekeeper thought for a few seconds. "Occasionally!"

Andrew nodded. "There must be a pattern. Pinpoint where it appears and try to track it and work out its pattern. Then plot its future moves until you can predict when it will arrive at its original position." Everyone turned and looked at Andrew.

"But it's random!" The Gatekeeper explained.

Andrew looked across at Agnes for verification as he spoke. "Surely if a thing lands in exactly the same place more than once it cannot be random. Therefore there must be a pattern."

Agnes thought the idea over. The man had a point. Whether or not it was correct was neither here nor there. It was an idea and, as she couldn't come up with a better one, it was the only one they had.

112

"Let's go to the place and wait for it to re-appear." She said.

Andrew looked at her. "That could be days, weeks, months. We've no idea when it will reappear."

Agnes smiled. "You're forgetting Andrew, time doesn't exist here."

His mouth fell open as the ramifications of what she had said began to sink in. The Gatekeeper looked at him. "If you are thinking along the lines of, if time doesn't exist how does a thing appear and disappear, I'd stop it right now. Trust me, thinking like that leads to madness. Just accept that things happen and we've no idea why."

Agnes stood up. "Come on then. No time like the present. Take us to the position of the rogue gateway."

The Gatekeeper rose and walked out from behind his desk. "Follow me!"

They did, out of the room, down the staircase, across the hall and through a small door. It opened onto a short corridor and led into a kitchen area. The Gatekeeper ignored everything and walked through the kitchen to another door. He held it open as the others filed out to find themselves outside, standing in a cobbled courtyard. Across from them was a small stable block. Between them, in the middle of the yard was a round table over which was a sunshade.

"That appeared from nowhere as well!" The Gatekeeper commented.

He walked across the yard to a large wooden gate set into a high stone wall. He pulled the gate open to reveal the familiar barren landscape. He pointed down. There were a series of large cuts and gouges set into the hard earth. Barely discernible against the grey surface was a broken metal frame.

Agnes peered down at it and wriggled her fingers. The broken metal began to move and shift as the frame began to un-break and reconstruct itself in front of their eyes. When it was complete it stood as a seven foot high and three feet wide oval shape with some ornate decorative pattern work around its edges.

Agnes looked at the Gatekeeper. "You only had one job! How did it get in that condition?"

The Gatekeeper shrugged. "There are very many gateways." He said defensively and then added, " I can't get around to every one of them!"

Agnes raised an eyebrow as she looked at him. "You mean there might be other rogue gateways out there?"

The Gatekeeper looked sheepish as he gave a slight shake of his head. "No. When this happened I checked them all. The rest are all in position and fully functional."

"But if there isn't any time, how can something age. More to the point how did...."

Agnes lifted her hand. "Andrew, remember what our friend here said. The more you go down that route the more you'll just jumble your mind. Just accept that here, wherever here is, things happen."

"Sometimes the only reason is that there is no reason!" George said.

Agnes gave him a one of her special looks. "Were you a philosopher?" She asked.

George shook his head. "I can't remember. I did have a butterfly collection though!"
115

"A lepidopterist!" Agnes remarked.

George looked confused. "I think I was English!"

Agnes shook her head. "One step forward, another step back." She muttered to no one in particular. She stepped up to the frame and began to run her hand over the metal. As she moved her hand the greyness seemed to slide from it and the metalwork began to shine. Then it glowed. Then it glowed some more. She was about to tell everyone to step back when she became aware of a shuffling noise behind her. She turned around to find that everyone had retreated back to the wall and George was in the act of opening the gate.

Before she could tell them not to worry, the ground beneath her feet began to shake and the frame filled with a huge ball of lightning. It flashed and crackled. The static shot out and Agnes became aware that her hair was standing on end. In front of her a large black void was filling the frame. She moved her arms and sparks flew from her finger tips. For a brief second it appeared as if a giant net had fallen over the frame. There was a fizzing sound and the net dissolved. Agnes lowered her arms. She felt the sweat dripping from her forehead. It had been a very difficult spell. Behind

116

her she heard the shuffling noise again as the group moved from the wall closer to the gateway. Suddenly a white face appeared in the frame. It moved forward slowly, its eyes flashing from one side to another. Agnes rummaged in her pocket and the orb appeared. Inside she could see the white faces thrashing around, mouths wide open with their silent screams. There was a popping sound and the face shot out of the gateway and disappeared inside the orb where it joined the others. She gave it a tap and replaced the orb in her pocket. She was about to look smug when she realised that the others were all looking at her and trying their best not to laugh. She wondered what was amusing them when she remembered her hair. She placed her hand on the top of her head and it settled back into its usual style, if the word style could be used to describe her hair. She gave a cough and gave them all a look as if to challenge them to say anything.

"Quiet a hair raising experience!" George commented. He hadn't realised what her look meant. For a second Agnes considered turning him into a frog.

"Now you have the gateway what do you intend doing with it?" The Gatekeeper asked.

"We're going to return to our own place and time!"
Andrew said and took a step towards the black
void. Agnes reached out and grabbed him by his
coat collar.

"That might not be a good idea!" She remarked.
The Gatekeeper nodded his head. "Just because it's
held here is meaningless. There's no telling where
it might lead to."

Chastened Andrew took a step backwards, and
looked towards Agnes. She shrugged. "It might or
it might not, I'm not sure, but there's better ways
of finding out than diving head first into it."

She glanced across to Marmaduke who had drawn
his pistol and was pointing it at the centre of the
void. "And I'm not sure sending a ball in there is a
very good idea. Supposing you shot an innocent
party?"

Marmaduke lowered his pistol. Agnes turned back
and stared into the blackness. As she turned
Marmaduke lifted his pistol once again. Innocent
party or not, he wasn't taking any chances. Agnes
reached into her pocket, rummaged around and
pulled out a handful of dried beans. She glanced
down and counted them. There were five. Gently
she tossed them into the void.
118

Beside her the Gatekeeper gave a scornful snort. "Now I've seen everything. Magic beans? This isn't Jack and the Beanstalk."

Agnes turned to him. "Never underestimate the power of magic beans." She said with a twinkle in her eye. As she spoke tentacles of green came creeping out of the mouth of the void. The Gatekeeper gave a little giggle. Then the tentacles dug into the grey earth, rooting and fixing themselves.

Agnes turned back to all of them. "Yes it's a type of bean, but its holding both ends of the void together. In short by using the beans as a sort of rope I've managed to get both ends of the void stabilised!"

"But we don't know where the other end is fixed!" The Gatekeeper observed.

"Let's find out!" Agnes replied and with that she stepped into the gateway. This time she didn't fall, she stepped out onto a large green branch and onto a patch of grass. As she looked around she became aware that the others had followed her.

Marmaduke was still holding his pistol in his hand.
119

Andrew stood with his eyes wide open. George just stood there.

"Where are we?" Andrew asked.

Agnes turned around. "I do wish you'd stop asking. It's obvious, we're somewhere else!"

Andrew was about to say something but Marmaduke put his hand on his arm and shook his head. Andrew shut up and continued looking at the landscape.

They were in what seemed to be the heart of an English countryside, standing in a grass meadow complete with colourful wild flowers, surrounded by green hedgerows and trees. Small birds flew in the air and darted in and out of the trees. In the near distance was a strange structure. It was a tall thin tower complete with arms that slowly turned as the wind blew. It was a windfarm, or at least one of the windmills that windfarms are made from. Agnes took the sight in and sent out a feeler, just to sense the immediate surroundings. She realised they were somewhere around the start of the 21st century. The single windmill told her that. There was a noise in the distance. She looked across the field. A motor car was speeding along a county lane. Georges face lit up as he pointed towards it

"Is this the future?" he asked.

"I'm afraid it is!" Agnes answered. "We're not only in the wrong place, we're in the wrong time."

Agnes allowed her senses to roam around the field. At the far end stood a herd of cows. She continued her scan but her senses caused her to turn back to the cows. There was something not quite right with them. They seemed, well they seemed just not right. She concentrated and stared hard at the one standing nearest to her. She blinked. The creature wasn't a creature. It was a machine, a machine that seemed to be growing actual flesh. A meat machine.

"What in all that's holy is that?" They all turned to see Andy pointing over their heads. They looked to where he was pointing to see that the noise was coming from a small dot in the sky that was growing bigger by the minute. Agnes turned her attention away from the mechanical cows. "It's called a helicopter." She said.

"There's another." George said.

"And another behind that." Marmaduke added.

Agnes looked as the small fleet. They were heading straight for them. A seventh or eighth sense made her circle her arm and a large protective screen surrounded them all. Before anyone could react the lead helicopter sprayed the ground in front of them with a burst of high velocity bullets. In front of them the ground sprang up in small explosions of grass and earth. Instinctively everyone ducked. Marmaduke tried to speak but his voice was drowned out by the cackle of a loudspeaker relaying an automatic voice.

"Intruders. Do not move!"

In the background the remaining helicopters came in to land, their blades causing a wind to blow around the protective screen. Within a few seconds a small army of heavily armed men dressed in black uniforms and hoods began to disgorge from the machines and race towards them.

Marmaduke looked at the pistol in his hand and looked at the firepower aimed towards him. He gave a nervous glance towards Agnes. She raised and arm and pointed at the ground the men were about to cross. It suddenly burst into flames. The men stopped as quickly as they could. Some even threw themselves to one side to avoid running into the flames. Some couldn't stop in time and ran through the flames only to roll on the ground to try to extinguish the flames burning their uniforms. A helicopter overhead let lose another salvo of heavy gunfire this time aimed directly at the group. The bullets hit the protective screen and ricocheted all over the place. Some flew back through the flames and hit the attackers.

Agnes moved her arms again and a black cloud appeared. There was a rumble of thunder and a bolt of lightning hit one of the grounded helicopters. It exploded in a mass of flame and shattered rotor blades. Electricity fizzed and crackled in the air and affected the mechanical cows that suddenly came to life and charged the remaining helicopters, the troopers and the flames.

Then a voice could be heard. "I suggest you step backwards. The void has become unstable again!"

Without hesitation they all took a step backwards into the black circle and found themselves on a large tanglement of green. Then they were back on the grey desert.

The Gatekeeper was standing to one side of the framed void. "I'd advise you all to take one step to the left!" he said.

They did as he suggested. Just in time as a large brown shape came hurtling out of the void. They watched as it righted itself and set off at a steady cantor heading for the horizon.

"Just what was that?" The Gatekeeper asked, watching as it disappeared into the distance.

"The future!" Andrew remarked.

Agnes turned her head towards him. "Someone's future. Not ours I'm glad to say!" She turned back to the Gatekeeper. "It didn't work, we didn't return to the house."

The Gatekeeper gave a shrug of his shoulders. "I never thought magic beans would."

Agnes gave a slight stamp of her foot. "Of course they weren't magic beans. I cast as strong a holding spell as I could. In theory it should have held the void stable at both ends. The magic beans were just a little embellishment."

The Gatekeeper looked blank.

"A joke!" Agnes sighed.

The Gatekeeper tried a smile. "Oh, a joke. I see now. But anyway I did warn you. You didn't know where the other end was did you? Are you sure this "let's find out as we go along" policy is the right one?"

"Have you any better ideas?" Agnes asked rather tartly.

"Just how many worlds do these gateways lead to?" Andrew asked as he brushed bits of mud and grass from his jacket.

The Gatekeeper gave another shrug. "Infinite!" he replied.

Andrew let out a groan. "We're stuck here forever!" He wailed.

Agnes shook her head. "There is no time!" She said.

Before anyone could reply there was a popping sound and a small unidentified little creature fell from the void. It's startled eyes looked anxiously around before it scampered off towards a large rock and proceeded to dig under it.

"Just what I need, rats!" The Gatekeeper said.

"It was a gerbil." George observed watching as the little creature disappeared under the rock.

Agnes turned towards him. "How did you know that?" She asked.

He shook his head. "No idea. Will they really have flying cars in the future?" he asked.

Agnes nodded absent mindedly. "I have an idea!" she suddenly said.

No one knew whether to be delighted, happy, worried or just plain scared. Agnes smiled "Trust me!"

They all settled on being worried. She turned to George. "Can you bring your car around to here?" She asked pleasantly. George nodded.

After a few seconds in which George just stood smiling Agnes gave a little sigh. "Will you please bring your car around here?"

The penny dropped and George set off at a little trot until he disappeared around the corner of the house. No one said anything and stayed where they were until they heard the sound of the approaching motor. George was in the driving seat and next to him, in the passenger seat, was the little man they knew as a Wally.

As he drove up and cut the engine George looked down at Agnes. "The little chappie says he knows the way so I thought I'd better bring him along!"

The Gatekeeper looked at the little man. "How do you know the workings of the void?"

The little man sat and thought very hard before giggling and saying "Hide and seek."

Agnes looked puzzled and cast a little spell to see if the little man was speaking the truth, or at least the truth as he knew it. "What do you hide and what do you seek?" She asked.

The a puzzled look crossed little man's face. "Each other!" he replied.

Then she had one of those ideas. The type of idea that is so outside the box, that the box not only can't be seen, it doesn't even exist.

"What do you know about the ruins where the palace once stood?"

The little man blinked. Behind her the Gatekeeper gave out a gasp. "The Temple? Have you seen the Temple?"

Agnes ignored him and concentrated on the little man. "Who lived there?"

The little man blinked again. "The Lordly Ones!" he said in a very quiet voice.

There was a shuffling behind her. She turned to see the Gatekeeper trying to slip back into the house. He had been stopped by Marmaduke who held his pistol at his head. The Gatekeeper help up both his hands.

"What do you know about the Lordly Ones?" Marmaduke growled.

The Gatekeeper lowered his arms. Marmaduke snarled and gave the pistol a little squeeze. The Gatekeeper raised his arms again. "You do know that in a timeless place a bullet will not fire out of the barrel." He said.

"Let's find out!" Marmaduke said and pulled the trigger.

The Gatekeeper dropped a hand and the bullet stopped in mid air, inches away from his face. He smiled.

"I stopped it!" he said.

"No you didn't!" Agnes remarked.

The Gatekeeper looked at her from out of his cowl. "I did!"

Agnes shook her head "Take a closer look!"

The Gatekeeper looked in front of him at the bullet frozen in mid air. It had come to a stop against an invisible shield.

"Now look behind the bullet." Agnes suggested. The Gatekeeper looked. There was the outline of another shield, one with a hole drilled right through its centre.

"Guess which one was mine!" Agnes said. If the Gatekeeper had been smiling he wasn't now.

"The Lordly Ones!" She repeated.

The Gatekeeper lowered his head. "We do not speak of them. They were here at the beginning.
129

They were the creators."

Andrew looked around at the desert and the barren landscape. "They didn't make a very good job of things!" He remarked.

The Gatekeeper gave a scornful snort. "What do you know? Once there were temples and gardens, ornamental pools and fountains, trees and blue skies."

"What went wrong?" Agnes asked.

"Rivalries broke out between them. Faction turned on faction. Eventually only a handful of them survived the plotting and assassinations. By then the gardens had fallen into disrepair. There were not enough people to maintain them. As their power faded the desert reclaimed its lands." He paused and looked out over the dead landscape. "Eventually the ones who remained sealed themselves in the palace and surrounded themselves with spells and incantations, not trusting their own followers and guards."

Agnes held up her hand. "You mean to say the Lordly Ones were magicians?"

The Gatekeeper shook his head. "They were more

than that. They were the creators."

Agnes raised an eyebrow as her mind worked overtime. Just who were these people, and more to the point, what did they create? By the look on everyone's face she realised that she had spoken the words aloud.

"They sound a bit of a rum lot if you ask me!" George remarked.

The Gatekeeper turned to him and his voice took on a harsh tone. "They were the Lordly Ones!"

"Sounds to me they were a bunch of magicians that fell out." Andrew observed. "Fell, out, declared war on each other and wiped themselves out!" He added.

Agnes turned towards him "But did they?"

"Of course they did. They existed eons ago You have seen the ruins for yourself, they are ancient." The Gatekeeper replied.

Agnes smiled. "I thought time didn't exist here!"

The Gatekeeper looked down at the ground. "It stopped when the last of the Lordly Ones vanished!" he muttered.

"How did you get here?" Andrew asked suddenly.

"The Gatekeeper shrugged. "I have always been here."

"You can't have. If you've always been here you would have seen the palace for yourself." Andrew said.

"Perhaps it was just legend!" Marmaduke added. As he spoke he placed the pistol in his other hand. The conversation was going on and his arm was beginning to ache.

The Gatekeeper noticed the movement and made a step towards the house. Before he could take a second step he heard a click behind his ear. He turned. Andrew was holding another pistol at him. He looked at Agnes.

She shrugged. "Don't look at me. I'm not in charge. They are their own men who make their own decisions." She snapped her fingers and the bullet fell to the ground and rolled towards the Gatekeepers feet.

"Anyway it can't be legend. I've seen the ruins myself." She looked a little more closely at the Gatekeeper. You never answered the question. If you have always been here why didn't you see the palace?"

The Gatekeeper seemed to ignore the question. He stood there in silence looking from one to the other. They waited for an answer but it wasn't forthcoming. Instead the figure leant forward and pulled the cowl back revealing a head and face that resembled a skull more than it did a living face. Set inside the skull were two eyes of startling blue.

"Just what are you?" Agnes asked.

The Gatekeeper turned towards her and opened its mouth. No sound came out of it. Instead a succession of dry grunts and clicks emerged. The figure turned and took one step back to the house, then stopped and took a step backwards. Then it began to walk in a very tight circle, then it fell over and remained stationary on the grey dusty ground. Marmaduke looked towards Agnes. She took a step forward and bent down to examine the figure. She pulled the cloak to one side to reveal a part of the body. There were gasps of surprise from all of them. Agnes looked up.

"It's not human. It's mechanical!"

George jumped down from his motorcar. "It's a robot!" he exclaimed.

Andrew looked at Agnes, there was a hint of panic in his voice. "What's a robot?" he asked.

"A mechanical man!" Marmaduke replied, still holding his pistol, only now he was pointing it at the ground.

"Now that's odd!" Agnes said.

"I should say so!" George agreed.

Then they all heard a high pitched squeal. They turned to look at the Wally who was beginning to speak. He gave a little giggle and looked up at Agnes.

"They made him. They created him and his kind to guard the portals. It was their task. They were the original gatekeepers but they created these mechanical things to look after them on their behalf as they warred with each other."

Agnes turned towards him. "When you say they...."
134

"The Lordly Ones." He replied.

Andrew knelt down and examined the humanoid figure lying on the desert floor. "Is it dead?"

Agnes shook her head. "I'm not too sure it was alive in the first place." She reached out a hand and passed it over the contraption. "Let's just say its ceased to function."

Andrew stood up and wiped the grey dust from his breeches. "What do we do now?"

Agnes paused to think as all eyes turned to her. She gave a little self conscious shrug. "We could stick to the original plan, but now we have options."

"Which are?"Andrew asked, which wasn't an unreasonable question, all things considered.

"We have two. Option one is that we hop onto Georges car and try to find a way through the void."

She paused. No one said anything so she continued. "The second option is to have a look at those ruins and try to find out more about the

Lordly Ones. There are secrets here and I don't like secrets."

George climbed back into the driving seat. "No time like the present. Hop on!"

Agnes gave him one of her special looks. Had George intended to make a joke she asked herself. Surely in a timeless place the only time was the present. She shook her head. Forget about the time thing she reminded herself. Then a penny appeared at the back of her mind and began to drop. She turned to the Wally. "If you have no memory, how do you know about the Gatekeeper?" She nodded towards the mechanical man. It had slipped and its arms were now poking out at odd angles.

The little man tapped his forehead with his index finger. "It comes back. From where I know not!"

Marmaduke gave a cough and nudged the mechanical body with his foot. "If it was a mechanical thing how did it first appear as the ghost of a headless Elizabethan gentleman?"

Agnes looked at him. "That is a very good question. I have to admit it hadn't crossed my mind. If I say it was an illusion created by the mechanical being I would have to admit it had some sort of magical powers. That means it could think for itself." She paused as she thought the question through before adding "But if it had its own powers, why did it fall over and cease functioning."

"Flat battery?" George offered.

Before anyone could ask what a battery was Agnes clicked her fingers. "By George, I think you may have something there, only not an electrical battery, but some sort of magical battery."

"Why here and why now?" Andrew asked.

"It just ran out!" George replied.

"But if it ran out that means it must be subject to some sort of time!"

Agnes turned to Andrew. Sometimes she was surprised at the sharpness of his brain. Then she realised in his business a sharp brain was essential if you were to remain one step ahead of the Excise men.

"Good point!" she said. "Even more to the point, where would he get it recharged?"

The Wally clapped its hands. "The ruins!" he said.

"How do you know?" Agnes asked.

The Wally sat, closed its eyes and thought hard, then it looked up at Agnes with its eyes wide open.

"I have seen them walking there and returning. Not often, but I have seen them."

Agnes didn't hesitate. "Right, to the ruins, oh, and bring his nibs along. Let's see if we can get him back onto his feet again."

They lifted the broken mechanical and placed it into the car boot. Then, as they piled aboard the vintage car Agnes wriggled her fingers. The engine turned on and George moved the gear stick. As the vehicle moved forward there was a popping sound. Suddenly at either side, the car sprouted small, fin like wings and lifted into the air.

George looked down at the ground retreating below him. "I say! That's rather jolly!"

He put his foot on the accelerator and the car shot forward though the air. Marmaduke and Andrew said nothing but hung on. Agnes closed her eyes and enjoyed the wind passing through her hair. The
138

Wally pointed a trembling finger towards the distant horizon. George turned the wheel slightly and the Wally nodded through gritted teeth. He wasn't too sure about this flying thing.

Chapter Six

The air around them seemed to blur and then clear once more. The Wally began to chatter and point towards a large outcrop of rock. George turned the steering wheel and brought the car gently to the ground and stopped. He turned towards Agnes. "Please tell me that was magic."

Agnes nodded. George patted the side of the car fondly. "Thank goodness for that. I didn't think the old girl could hold together much longer at that sort of speed."

There was a crunching noise as Marmaduke and Andrew stepped onto the ground. Marmaduke sniffed the air and felt the hairs on the nape of his neck begin to rise. Something wasn't right. Andrew looked at Marmaduke, read the signs and pulled his pistol from his belt. George was oblivious being fully occupied by looking at the dials on his dashboard and shaking his head. The Wally had ducked down and was hiding under the car.

Agnes had noticed something as well. She looked at the desert floor. They had arrived at it from
140

another direction so she didn't recognise it at first, then she let her mind roam. She soon found a set of her own footprints and followed them. The she saw the series of stones set in lines. It was the foundations of the temple and they were glowing. Before she could say a word the earth trembled and shook. Then, bursting out from the underground, the temple began to emerge. Earth and loose rock began tumbling through the air.

Agnes moved her hand and an invisible bubble of protection appeared around them. Soil and lose ground showered down over it. In a few seconds it was all over. They looked up. Standing in front of them was the temple Agnes had seen in her vision, only this time it was for real. The trees and ornamental bushes rippled in a slight breeze. The grass was soft and luxurious green, the golden paths, laid out in geometric patterns, led towards the entrance of the building. As they looked up at the walls they were forced to blink. They were shining, seemingly made of gold. The four towers reached up towards the sky which had now turned a bright and vibrant blue. Light shone and danced of the temples great, golden globe.

Agnes moved her arm and the protective screen disappeared, she peered under the car. "Have you ever seen that before?" She asked the Wally. His teeth were chattering so much he could only shake his head. Agnes stood upright and brushed the front of her skirts before looking at her companions.

"Someone has gone to a lot of trouble to get us here. It would be downright rude of us not to pay them a visit."

She took a step forward, then stopped. Something was approaching. It was flat and floated through the air at head height. When it reached them it lowered itself to the ground. It was a large Persian carpet. Agnes looked down at it, she could feel a strange and powerful magic seeping out if it.

"It's a magic carpet!" Andrew exclaimed.

"Door to door service!" Agnes observed.

They all stepped onto it and sat down crossed legged. Agnes remained standing. "I think you're meant to sit down on it." George remarked.

"If I get down there there's a grave danger that I'll not get up again. I don't do cross legged!"

As she spoke a chair appeared out of nowhere. Agnes looked at it and realised the word chair hardly described the seat in front of her. It was more like a small golden throne with bright red cushions. She smiled and settled herself into its luxury.

"What about him?" George asked pointing towards the Wally who was still hiding underneath the car.

"Would you like to come with us?" Agnes asked.

The little man shook his head so violently that he was in danger of knocking himself out on the exhaust pipe. "Cannot go in there." The words could just be made out amongst the noise of his chattering teeth.

"In which case could you keep an eye on the car please?"

The little man nodded his head. "Oh and keep an eye on the mechanical thing in the boot." She added as she sat back in the chair.

They sat there in silence for a few minutes before George commented. "Aren't you meant to say some magic words?"

Before she could reply a voice spoke some sort of incantation and the carpet gently rose in the air and
143

flew across the gardens towards the large double door at the entrance to the temple.

"It is going to stop, isn't it?" Andrew asked anxiously as the carpet flew nearer and nearer to the doors. Then, just as it seemed they were about to crash, both doors silently swung open and the carpet flew into a large cathedral like space, before stopping and gently floating onto a mosaic floor.

Everyone stood up and stepped off the carpet. Once it was free of its passengers it rose and disappeared into the dome high above them.

"It's like St Pauls Cathedral!" George exclaimed. "You remember St Pauls then!" Agnes remarked. George blinked. "I suppose I do. No idea when I was there, or why for that matter."

Their attention was attracted by a door opening and a figure appeared. It was a large clean shaven man dressed in a golden turban and waistcoat pulled over a huge bronze body. A thick brocade cummerbund was strapped around a very large stomach. Below the belt he was wearing a pair of golden pantaloons. His feet were encased in a pair of heavily brocaded slippers that curled up at the toes.

144

"It's straight out of the Arabian Nights!" George exclaimed.

"No its not!" Agnes contradicted. She moved her hand and the air around the man shimmered. The gold dissolved along with the bronzed physique. In its place stood a small man who looked very similar to the Wally they had left behind, although this man was better groomed. He blinked and looked around him. He opened his mouth to speak but the voice that emerged was more suited to his previous incarnation. "You are requested to follow me to a room where you may refresh yourselves," it said.

The voice didn't match the figure and Marmaduke looked around just to make sure that no one else had spoken.

Once he had greeted them the man turned around and walked with as much dignity as he could down a long, high and broad passageway.

"He's naked!" Andrew observed.

"It's the worst case of the Emperor's new clothes I've ever come across!" Agnes replied.

They followed the figure, trying hard not to stare at

the short legs and wobbly bottom that preceded them. It was difficult. The figure turned and opened a door they hadn't noticed. It stood to one side to allow them to enter. As they passed him each one deliberately kept looking straight ahead.

Once inside they found themselves in a smallish room. Decorative wall hangings and tapestries hung from the walls. The floor was strewn with patterned rugs and large brocade cushions. Ottomans were spread around a large table embellished and inlaid with gold. In the centre of the table were a series of platters on which fruits and sweetmeats were piled. Jugs of wine stood next to four sparking glasses. They all turned to Agnes. She closed her eyes for a second and opened then again.

"Everything you see is real, but I'd be careful of the bananas, they look a bit green to me." She remarked.

"What's this?" Marmaduke asked poking a finger at a pile of jelly squares covered in a fine white powder.

"Turkish delight!" Agnes replied.

Marmaduke picked it up, sniffed at it, and put
146

some in his mouth, then pulled it out again. "It's too sweet and clogs up my teeth. He said replacing it on the side of his plate.

"Try the cous cous!" A voice behind them said.

They turned to see a figure dressed in a large white robe. The hood was pulled up so the face was hidden. The sleeves were large and hung low hiding the figures hands. Agnes raised her fingers. The figure looked at her. "I am neither illusion, nor mechanical."

Agnes nodded. "And you're not a man either, at least not in the human sense of the word."

The figure laughed. "I am an elemental. I am one of those they call The Lordly Ones."

Agnes picked up a grape and gave it a quick examination before popping it into her mouth. She bit it between her back teeth. It was sweet and had no pips. Everyone watched as she swallowed. She ran her tongue around her mouth and turned to the hooded figure. "You have certainly gone to great lengths to get me here, why?"

The Lordly One opened his arms. "Please be seated. Help yourself."

Again all eyes turned to Agnes. She gave a slight nod. Everyone found somewhere to sit. Once they were all settled the figure continued speaking.

"The rogue portal was not of our doing. It happened. The one we appointed Gatekeeper failed in its task. It became distracted, he was deactivated. Another will be sent in its place. It spent too much time in the haunted house."

Agnes shook her head. "He's in the boot of our car. You can recharge him. Anyone can make a mistake. Rest assured he won't do that again."

The Lordly One gave a slight bow. "As you wish, but I will be keeping a very close eye on him."

"He was a good illusionist. The headless ghost was quiet a trick."

The Lordly One laughed. "Do you really think..." he paused and gave Agnes a deep stare. "You didn't think it was capable of that. You knew a greater force was at work."

Agnes shrugged. It didn't matter if she'd believed it was capable of magic or not. The figure in front of her believed it so that must be the truth.

"When did you become aware we had travelled through the portal?"

"From the moment we positioned the portal in the Scarborough house!" The figure replied.

"But I thought you said that the portal had gone rogue. That its appearance and disappearance was chance?" Agnes looked across at Andrew. She was impressed. Despite the surreal environment he was still ahead of the situation.

The Lordly One stepped across the room towards the table and helped himself to a piece of Turkish delight. He turned towards Marmaduke.

"You're right. It is a bit sweet!" he swallowed and returned his gaze at Agnes. "There's nothing wrong with an elemental enjoying his food!"

"I never said there was!" Agnes replied.

"You haven't answered my question!" Andrew said.

The hooded figure picked up a large piece of melon, examined it and replaced it on the plate. "The portal was rogue, but once it was stable it would always return to where it had been placed, whatever the time period."

"You mean to say that you deliberately placed it in the 21st century to attract my attention?" Agnes asked.

The hooded figure nodded as it sat and stretched itself out on an ottoman holding a plateful of grapes. Agnes watched as a grape disappeared into the darkness of the hood. "But when it became unstable it began passing through time, in the same place."

The figure slowly shook its head. "If only. Oh no! When it went rogue, it went really rogue. It passed through both time and different dimensions. You've been there. Once you pass through it you've no idea where or when it will return."

"Hasn't Agnes fixed that particular problem? The last time I saw it the thing looked pretty fixed to me!" Marmaduke suddenly said. He was getting a bit grumpy. He didn't like fruit and could still feel the Turkish delight sticking to his teeth.

The Lordly One looked across at him. "One end is fixed. Let's put it like this. You've nailed the tail of a snake to the ground, but the head is still threshing about."

"So what is so important that you'd risk bringing us here, even though the portal was faulty?" Agnes asked. She too was getting a bit grumpy. She thought she was being patronised and she didn't like that. Also she wasn't too fond of being put in danger.

"It wasn't unstable when we did it!" The Lordly One replied.

"But....!" Andrew began.

Agnes cut him off. "It's a time thing!" She explained.

"There is no time and therefore there is all the time!" The Lordly One added.

Andrew leant back in his seat. His head was beginning to hurt.

"Why? Agnes repeated.

"I want you to stop a war!" The hooded figure replied.

Chapter Seven

The room fell silent. Agnes could feel everyone's eyes looking at her. She blinked and sent out a small probing spell towards the Lordly One. It stopped halfway across the room. The figure lifted its head and raised its hands. Then it pulled the hood from its head revealing a white face surrounded by golden hair. The face was of a timeless age, delicate and in perfect proportions. Despite his lack of religion Andrew found himself crossing himself. "You're an angel!" he proclaimed.

The face smiled. "Angelic yes. Angel no!"

Marmaduke broke the moment. "What war?" he asked. Now there was a prospect of fighting he had regained interest in the conversation.

"The war we are about to fight! The war between us Lordly Ones!"

Agnes shuffled in her seat. "But that war has already been fought, and lost!"

"It has been fought, but yet here and now, it has yet to happen!"

Agnes gave her head a scratch. "But I cannot alter events. I have seen the result of your war, the ruins and the desolation of your landscape."

The Lordly One stretched. "You have seen one reality. Now you will help create another!"

Now even Agnes was beginning to get confused with when and where they were. "Why me?"

"You came highly recommended!" The Lordly One replied with a smile.

"Who by?" She was curious.

"By someone you've yet to meet!" The Lordly One replied.

Now Agnes's head was beginning to hurt. She put her fingertips to her forehead and gave it a slight massage. "How am I supposed to do this?" She asked hoping the throbbing would go away.

"We have to explain to the different factions that a war would not be a good idea."

"How many are there?" Marmaduke asked.

153

"Factions or Lordly Ones?" The Lordly One asked in reply.

"Both!" Marmaduke and Agnes replied together.

The elemental looked around the room. "There are five of us, each in separate factions!" he replied.

"So, only four others!" Marmaduke observed.

"What is the cause of the argument?" Agnes asked.

The figure looked across to the tapestry hanging on the wall. "The shape of the gardens.!" He replied.

Everyone fell silent.

"What the...." Andrew exclaimed eventually as it sunk in.

"One wants a round garden, the other wants a square one. Another wants a water feature. The fourth wants a series of trees planted in neat lines, then another wants a series of hedges, then the other wants crazy paving, then one wants an ornamental lake, another wants a rockery, another, and on it goes."

"I thought there were only four of them!" George

asked.

"There are. You see how difficult the situation is." The elemental replied.

"Where are they now?" Agnes asked glancing around the room, just in case.

The elemental laughed. "They all stormed out of the palace and created four fortresses. From there they began to gather their forces. Now they sit on the four corners of the square with their armies ready to march."

"Where are they marching to?" Marmaduke asked.

"To the centre of the square!" was the reply.

"And where is this square? Agnes asked, although she had a feeling she already knew the answer.

"Here!" the elemental replied.

"How long will it be before they begin their march?" Andrew asked. He was now sitting forward, as far as he was concerned the conversation was taking a turn for the worse.

The elemental ignored him but looked at Agnes.

"They have already marched. In one reality they are camped outside the palace walls. In another reality they have already destroyed the palace."

"What about here and now?" Agnes asked.

"Their camps can be seen in the distance." Came the answer.

"I need to see for myself." She replied and picked up a silver dish. She emptied the apricots out of it and as they rolled across the table she picked one up and dropped it into her pocket. Everyone watched as she poured some water into the dish, reached into her pocket and pulled out some herbs and spices which she sprinkled over the surface of the water. She allowed the water to bubble and then, as it settled, she peered into it.

The view she saw was looking down onto the palace. At each corner of the building, equally spread a short march away, were the lights of campfires. She moved her hand and hovered over one. She blinked, and then blinked again. Then she moved her hand to look at the other camps. Then she sat back and looked up to the elemental.

"Just where do they do their recruiting?" She asked.

"They have all the time in the world." He replied.

Marmaduke stood up and walked across to Agnes's make shift scrying bowl and looked into the water. He found himself looking down on an army of Roman troops. Agnes clicked a finger and the scene changed to a view of a Viking Hoard. Another click and the scene changed to an army of Cossacks. Finally he found himself looking as an army of what seemed to be Japanese warriors.

"Wait until they start using armies from the 21st century!" The elemental sighed.

Agnes looked back into the scrying bowl. The armies were still evolving, as were the weapons. Armies of armour clad knights morphed into armies of musketeers that morphed into soldiers from the Napoleonic wars.

"An arms race!" She observed.

"When will it stop?" Andrew asked anxiously.

"When one of them decides it has the upper hand!" The elemental replied.

A sinking feeling began to grow in Agnes's stomach. It was an arms race and the first to evolve the ultimate deterrent just might not use it as a deterrent. Then she understood.

"They went nuclear!" She said.

The elemental nodded. Agnes gave him one of her special looks. "You have the power to stop time!" she said.

"There is no time!" he replied.

"In which case, unless we can find a way to slow down the evolution of those armies it will happen again!"

The elemental stood up and raised his arms in the air before beginning to chant in a strange and lingering language.

Agnes looked back into the bowl. The evolution had stopped. The elemental stopped chanting. "The four of them will know what I'm doing and break my spell. We all have equal power!"

Agnes smiled. "Ah, but you have me!" As she spoke she raised her arms. The air in the room sizzled. She lowered her arms and peered into the bowl.

"I've frozen them in time." She said and looked across to the elemental. "You can put your arms down now."

"They won't stay like that for long. They will find a way to break your spell."

"I'm hoping it will hold them until we can think of what to do next!" She replied.

"You mean you don't have a plan?" Andrew exclaimed.

Agnes paused in thought for a second. "Actually I might have."

She rummaged around in her pocket and pulled out the glass orb. She held it up for the elemental to see. He peered into it and then jerked his head back as a ghostly white face appeared and snarled at him.

"What is that?" he asked. It was apparent the sight had unsettled him

"You've never seen them before?"

The elemental looked at Agnes with horror.

"Them? You mean there's more than one of them?"

"Lots!" Agnes said and smiled a little smile.

"The elemental shuddered. "What are they?"

"Ghosts!" Andrew answered.

The elemental gave a nervous little laugh. "There are no such things as ghosts!"

"Explain that to them!" Marmaduke said nodding towards the orb.

The elemental looked into the orb again. The faces were darting around inside it. He took a step backwards. "Where have they come from?" he asked.

"The haunted house." Agnes replied.

Andrew had been looking into the scrying bowl and noticed something. "I think the armies are beginning to move again." He said.

Agnes stepped back to the bowl and looked into its waters, moving her hand to gain a closer look.

Andrew was right. Although they had ceased to evolve they were still moving closer towards them. She looked up at the elemental. "Our combined spell has stopped them evolving, but not from moving. They'll be here in a short while.

She turned to George. "We're going to need your motor car again, if you don't mind."

George stood up and made an exaggerated bow. "We are at your service madam."

She turned to the elemental. "You're coming along as well."

They walked through the corridors of the palace and left by the main door where they clambered aboard the car. It was a bit crowded to say the least, George was in the driving seat with Agnes as the front passenger. The Wally was squashed up in the foot well between her feet. She wasn't too happy about that but as Marmaduke, Andrew and the elemental filled up all the available space in the rear, there wasn't much option, especially as he refused point blank to stand on the running board.

The engine spluttered into life and the machine rose up. The air around it blurred and then cleared. Below them they could see a cloud of dust. At its head and responsible for creating the dust clouds were a dozen Centurion tanks from the second world war. Behind them marched an army of men dressed in leather armour and carrying long halberds with vicious point and glistening blades. Behind them was a platoon of Roman spear throwers. At each flank were cavalrymen that seemed to resemble a company of Indian Sepoys.

"Bit of a mixed bunch!" Agnes remarked.

"What are those?" Andrew asked pointing at the approaching tanks.

"Think of them as mounted cannon, only a lot more powerful and manoeuvrable." Agnes replied fumbling in her pocket. She pulled out her orb. "Now let's see if my idea is any good."

She muttered to herself before uttering a little incantation using words no one had ever heard before. She then lifted the orb into the air and passed her free hand over its surface. There was a popping noise and a slight flash before half a dozen white faces were suddenly flying around the orb. Agnes clicked her fingers and the heads seemed to split open allowing more and more heads to emerge. Soon the air was filled with the white things. She moved her hand once more and
162

the heads seemed to form into a pattern. They flew
around the orb once more and then headed off,
flying towards the advancing army.

"Do you think those things...."

Agnes cut the elemental off. "Watch!" was all she
said.

She moved her hand once more. Below them the
white heads suddenly grew in size. Now instead of
being small each of them was the size of a double
decker bus. When they were above the army they
began screaming. Everyone in the car slammed
their hands over their ears. The noise was so loud
that it drowned out the noise of the tanks and
caused the advancing troops to look up. They
didn't even have time to draw their weapons
before the giant white heads were among them,
darting in and out of their formation, causing them
to panic and step into each other. Some troops
weren't so lucky. The heads passed through them,
freezing them solid, leaving them to tumble to
earth where they were trampled by the rest of the
army whose one collective thought was to run. The
heads chased them. Within minutes the entire army
had dissipated, and scattered, running as fast as it
could back to its base with the heads following
close behind.

The elemental glanced at the carnage spread out before him. "The others are watching. They are weighing up whether or not they have an advantage."

Agnes slipped the orb back into her pocket. "Let's dissuade them from doing anything rash."

Hardly had she spoken the words when the sky lit up and the sound of an explosion could be heard in the distance. She nodded in its direction and George hit the accelerator.

Chapter Eight

Once again the car came to a stop high in the air
hovering above another moving army. It's make up
was remarkably similar to the one they had just
dispersed. Agnes took the orb out of her pocket
and once more produced half a down white heads.
She had just cast the repeat spell and released the
heads when she became aware of a buzzing in the
air. Everyone else heard it and they turned just in
time to see a biplane diving out of the sky, heading
directly towards them. Before anyone could say
anything the air was torn by the rat-tat-tat of a
Vickers machine gun. The plane was firing at
them. Agnes flicked a finger and created a shield.
The bullets hit it and bounced harmlessly off. The
plane continued its dive heading straight for them.
George hit the accelerator again only this time the
car didn't move. He glanced anxiously at Agnes, at
the approaching plane, and at his dashboard. He
pulled out the choke and hit the accelerator once
more. The engine gave a cough, but the car
remained stationary, hovering in the air. Then the
plane was on top of them.

To this day no one was quite sure of what
happened next. There was a roaring sound, a rush

of air, and then nothing. They all opened their eyes.

The plane was ahead of them with something standing on its wing. Agnes turned her head. Marmaduke wasn't in the car. They all watched as the plane pulled out of its dive and levelled up. The shape on the wing seemed to drop on all fours and move towards the cockpit where the pilot was trying, and failing, to keep the aircraft on an even path. The pilot then glanced towards the thing that was crawling along the wing towards him. It only took a second for him to make his mind up. Hitting a release button on his chest he stood up and jumped out of the plane. As he tumbled through the air there was a pop and a parachute burst out of the pack on his back. Then they all looked back at the plane. Marmaduke was standing in the cockpit as the plane began to lurch into a downwards spiral.

Agnes moved her hands. "Jump!" she shouted. Marmaduke jumped. He fell about twenty feet before bouncing into a large net that had appeared out of nowhere.

Suddenly the car started with a lurch. George steered it towards the net and brought it to a stop at its side. Andrew leant over and helped Marmaduke
166

climb back on board. There was a crash and an explosion as the plane hit the ground below. Then there was a second explosion.

George turned the car around. In the distance, where the army had been, the landscape seemed to be on fire. There was a second explosion, then a third. The second army was getting blown to bits.

"One of them has discovered rockets!" The elemental said with a shake of its head.

Agnes didn't say a word but reached up into the air and clenched her fist, then brought it down again until it pointed in the direction of where the rockets had been launched. Nothing happened for a short while. Then there was another explosion, bigger than the others. In the far distance the horizon seemed to burst into flames. Even from that distance they could feel the ground shake.

Agnes turned to the elemental. "Just the one army left."

She reached into her pocket and pulled out the orb. She stared at it in the palm of her hand, making sure that the ghosts inside were agitated, then she threw it. Everyone watched as the orb flew in the air. It didn't fall. Instead it continued flying through the air in a huge arc. They lost sight of it as it disappeared into the horizon. Then there was the sound of breaking glass.

Agnes turned to the elemental."Well now they have no armies left do you think we can get them to see sense?"

The elemental gave a shrug. "Who knows? We can but try."

Agnes turned to George. "If you would be so kind, please take us back to the palace."

Once again they all hung on as the car accelerated through the air, and once again they seemed to arrive as soon as they had set off.

They dismounted at the entrance to the Palace. As they walked into the huge hallway four clocked figures were waiting for them. The elemental turned to them. "Please wait here." he said and walked towards the figures. Everyone became aware of a distant humming in the air. They looked around to see where the sound was coming from.

"They are using some sort of telepathy to communicate with each other." Agnes said quietly.

Whatever the conversation was about it seemed to be heated. The humming grew louder, riding and falling, echoing around the dome over their heads. It seemed to go on for a long time before the elemental they knew turned around and walked back to them.

"They would like your opinion of the layout of the gardens." He said.

No one said anything. To say his remark was unexpected is to underestimate the use of the word underestimate.

"I need a large table!" Agnes replied.

The elemental nodded. "Follow me."

He led them all down a different corridor to a set of large doors that opened as they approached. They entered and found themselves in an enormous library. Books lined the walls as high as they could see. In the middle of the room was a large leather topped table with half a dozen ornately carved chairs positioned around it. Without waiting to be asked Agnes sat down first. The five elementals took the rest of the seats leaving Andrew, Marmaduke and George to stand.

Once again the Wally had refused to enter the building.

Agnes looked around her. "Right gentlemen, before we proceed would you all be good enough as to remove your hoods. Call me old fashioned but I like to see the faces I'm talking to."

The four hooded figures glanced at each other and as one raised their hands and pulled back their hoods. Agnes blinked. Someone, possibly Andrew let out an audible gasp. All five elementals were identical. It was impossible to tell one from the other. She regained her composure.

"Right gentlemen, to begin with, what is so important about the garden that would cause a war between you?"

Elemental one, as by numbering them as they sat around the table, was the only way Agnes could tell one from the other, began. "It is our sacred garden. It must be square."

Elemental two suddenly rose to its feet and slammed both hands on the table. "Heretic!" it shouted. "The garden must be curved!"

The third elemental was about to speak when

Agnes raised her hand in the air. "Decorum gentlemen, decorum!"

Elemental two turned to her. "Who are you to know the ways of the Lordly Ones? Our tradition states curves are essential."

Agnes gave it one of her special looks. The elemental stared back at her. Suddenly she felt a rush of power coming towards her. She placed her hand in front of her palm up. The air between the two of them crackled. The original elemental angrily turned around to face his counterpart. "You gave your word. You all gave your word. No violence."

Elemental two gave a divisive snort. "It was the witch, she started it. She sent a probe at me."

Elemental one tuned to Agnes. She raised her hands in an apology. "I apologise. It was unwise of me!"

The standing elemental looked down at her. "Do not think for one minute that your powers even come close to ours. We are elementals."

With that he raised his hands and a thunderclap

echoed around the room. Lightning danced and crackled over Agnes's head. She twitched a finger and a large metal rod appeared in the centre of the table. The lightning struck it. There was a flash and another crackle. The elemental just had time to duck as a streak of lightning flashed over his head.

"And I am Agnes!" She said noticing a scorch mark that had appeared on the far wall, behind the elementals head.

"Enough!" One of the elementals who hadn't spoken yet now spoke. "We agreed to allow her the opportunity to assist." He turned to the second elemental who was still standing. "It says much that you ignore an opportunity to alleviate our problem."

The second elemental gave a snarl.

"Warmonger!" The fourth suddenly screamed and a jet of blue light burst from its eyes and flared up on the chest of the standing elemental. The figure doubled up with the blow and was flung to the far side of the room. Within seconds the air was full of magic bolts and crackling beams of light

Marmaduke, Andrew and George dived under the table. Unseen Agnes reached into her pocket and pulled out the orb. Despite it appearing to be smashed over one of the approaching armies it was here and it was whole and it still contained some of the ghost heads. She cast a spell and the heads burst out, once again shattering the encasing glass. Then she followed the others under the table. Marmaduke looked at her. She put her finger to her mouth. "Wait!" she mouthed. Then the shrieking began.

The sound was similar to that of a popular firework known as "the serpent" gave out as it sent its showers of coloured sparks into the sky. It whizzed, crackled, but most of all shrieked. The noises were accompanied by the noise of magic.

"I say!" exclaimed George. The rest of them said nothing.

From under the table all they could see were the legs and feet of the elementals. At first glance it seemed as if they were engaged in some sort of strange dance. Suddenly a ghost head appeared and looked under the table. It gave a snarl and flew back up into the room. After a few minutes the room fell silent. Agnes popped her head out from under the table and looked around. Each of the warring elementals were standing with their backs firmly pinned in the corners of the room. Holding them were scores of white ghost heads. Every time an elemental moved the heads would dart at them, snapping, snarling and biting. Some even passed through their bodies causing the elementals to cry out and double up in pain.

Making sure the room was safe the four of them crawled out from under the table, watching as the elementals tried to beat the heads away.

"Now there's a thing!" Agnes exclaimed.

The first elemental addressed the others. "Brothers, I suggest the time for fighting and squabbling is over. Perhaps we can now get down to some serious discussions."

Elemental number three looked across the room towards Agnes. There was a deep hatred in its eyes. Then Agnes noticed something else. Behind the hatred was fear. She gave the slightest hint of a smile. "I have a solution!" She remarked.

Elemental number two let out a snort of derision. "How can the likes of you even pretend to offer such...."

Agnes twitched a finger and a ghost head suddenly swooped down and passed through the elementals
174

chest. It bent double with a gasp. "I do wish you would listen. It's far less painful." Agnes remarked as the elemental straightened up still holding its chest.

"Watch!" Agnes demanded. She turned towards the end of the table and moved her arms. A cloud of mist appeared and covered the surface. It glowed a little and then Agnes blew at it and it dispersed. As it cleared it revealed a model garden designed in neat geometrical shapes of triangles and squares. Before anyone could make a remark she repeated the movement. This time when the mist cleared a second garden appeared hovering over the first. This second one was designed in fluid, sweeping curves and circles. She moved her hands once again. This time a third layer appeared floating over the others. This design contained a series of small pools and lakes in the centre of which was a large fountain. Finally she revealed a fourth garden. This one looked as if it had come from the palace of a Japanese Emperor. It had rocks and areas of neatly groomed sand in sweeping curves and patterns. Grasses and ferns grew in ornamental pots. She stepped back to admire her work.

"Very clever!" The fourth elemental remarked sarcastically. "But which one will it be?"

"All of them!" Agnes replied.

The first elemental began to smile. Then he nodded. "As excellent solution!" he remarked. "Excellent!"

"Four gardens?"Andrew asked.

"Each in its own particular time!" The first elemental explained.

"Yes it's simple really. Each garden has been created in its own unique time!" Agnes said.

Andrew struggled with this. "But there is no time out there!"

"Exactly!" The elemental replied.

Andrew scratched his head. It was beginning to hurt again.

"Forget it. Just imagine that all four gardens exist at the same time in the same place." She said and then turned to the first elemental."You know how to achieve this?"

The elemental nodded and Agnes turned to address the other four. "Four gardens, one for each of you.

They will be constructed in your own time. However, as the other designs are so abhorrent to your sensitivities you will only have access to your own. You are forbidden from visiting each others."

The third elemental gave a grunt. But there are five of us. Where is the fifth garden?"

Agnes watched as a ghost head swooped down and just missed his face. The elemental jerked backwards. Agnes nodded towards the first elemental. "Our friend here will be the only one to have access to all four gardens. That way he will enjoy each design when he chooses." Then her voice turned stern. "And he will be able to keep an eye on you all, just to make sure you stick to the agreement."

"I haven't agreed to anything." One of them said. Agnes couldn't tell which one had spoken.

"But you will." She said and moved a finger. The ghost heads immediately surrounded them, darting in and out of their bodies. They all bent double and groaned.

"We agree!" they said as one.

"That's good! Now off you go. You're going to be

busy, you have gardens to create." Everyone in the room watched as one by one each of the four elementals slowly faded away until there was nothing left of them.

"Where have they gone?" Marmaduke asked.

"Each to their own time." The elemental replied.

"But there is no time!" Andrew muttered.

"Forget it!" Agnes and Marmaduke said together. The elemental looked up into the top corner of the room where the ghost heads had gathered. "Leave the window open. They'll find their own way back home!" Agnes said.

"Home?" He asked.

"Back to the haunted house." Agnes replied.

"It'll be a bit crowded in there!" George remarked.

"There's only the original dozen or so in there." Agnes said.

"But...."

"It's all done with mirrors!" Agnes replied.

Chapter Nine

"Of course we still have our problem of getting back to where we came from." Andrew said as they stood outside the palace.

"Ah yes the rogue portal!" The elemental remembered.

"I don't suppose you know how we do that?" Marmaduke asked.

The elemental shook its head. "I'm afraid most of our attention was taken up with arguing over the gardens. We just let the guardians look after them."

"So you let the guardians do the job for you?" Andrew asked.

The elemental grew slightly defensive. "We delegated. We were too busy attending our own problems."

Agnes tutted. "You mean arguing about gardens and going to war with each other. Tell me, just how long has all this been going on?"

"Since the end of time!" It replied.

Agnes wasn't going to be drawn into that one again. She gave a warning glance at Andrew and then turned back to the original point. "So the only things that know where the portals lead to are the guardians themselves?"

The elemental nodded.

"But you deactivated him, it!" Marmaduke snarled.

Agnes gave him a look. Marmaduke returned it with a look that said "but he did!"

Agnes turned back to the elemental. "So perhaps you would be so good as to reactivate him. Charge his batteries up again as it were."

Before he could answer George spoke up. "Go on old chap, play the game. One good turn deserves another!"

The elemental looked at him closely. "Just who are you again?"

George shrugged. "I'm not too sure about that old chap."

The elemental cocked its head. "Where have you come from?"

George made a gesture with his hand. "I seem to remember I fell through a hole in the road."

The elemental remained silent. He was thinking. Agnes turned to the rest of the group. "Could you get the Gatekeeper out of the boot please?"

Andrew and Marmaduke stood by as George opened the car boot. Carefully they lifted the robot out and placed it on the ground. When they had it laid out the elemental looked at it and then looked at Agnes. It lifted an arm so it was pointing towards the robot. A flash of light appeared and hit the Guardian in the chest.

Everyone took a step back and watched as the light sparkled and danced over the inert body. Slowly it came to life and very carefully stood up. It ran its hands over its body checking everything was alright. Then it straightened its robe and adjusted its cowl. It looked towards the elemental.

"Assist them in their return to their own place and time!" The elemental demanded.

"It will be done." It said.

The Guardian turned to look at Agnes. "Which particular time would you like to return to?"

Agnes looked at Marmaduke and then across to Andrew. The thought of the mayhem Andrew could create with even a little glimpse into the 21st century ran through her head. "The 18th century please. I can handle things from there." She replied to the Guardian.

"The eighteenth century it will be." It said and then vanished.

Everyone blinked. "Where the devil has he gone?" George asked.

"Back to the portal. He will be waiting for you there." The elemental replied.

"Are you coming?" Agnes asked.

The elemental shook its head. "No point. I wouldn't know what to do, where to look.

Agnes gave him a look. "Don't you think it's time you actually did what you're supposed to do instead of letting your Guardians do everything for you?"

The elemental gave her a look in return. "Perhaps that's what we are doing. Perhaps we were supposed to create the Guardians to do things on our behalf."

Agnes nodded. There really wasn't any answer to that. After all, when you are stood at the crossroads of infinite dimensions where time stands still, where everything that has happened is still happening, and everything that is yet to happen has already happened, well who was she to nit-pick. She just nodded her head and hoped she was giving the impression she knew what she was talking about.

"It's tricky!" The elemental explained. "Anyway I have four gardens to visit. Make sure everything is...."

"Rosy!" George said.

"Rosy, everything in the gardens is rosy." The elemental repeated. "Yes, oh I do hope one of them has planted roses. I do like roses."
With that he faded away.

Chapter Ten

The car came to a stop next to the portal at the rear of the haunted house. Standing next to it was the Guardian. Agnes turned towards him. Despite knowing it was actually a mechanical she still preferred to regard him as a male entity.

She pointed at the black void. "Before we even attempt to re-enter that thing theres just a few things I would like to discuss with you. Let's go back to the library. I could do with a sit down."

The Guardian lowered its head. "I thought you might say that. I have already prepared refreshments." He turned and led them back into the building.

"More fruit!" Marmaduke muttered under his breath.

"I managed to find some sardines!" The Guardian said without looking round.

Sure enough the Guardian was as good as his word. As they entered the library they could see the table was loaded with fresh bread, slices of beef and ham, cheeses of all types and flavours. A large jug of wine stood in the centre next to a pile of fruit.

"Cake!" remarked Agnes as she eyed a very large and very tempting Victoria sponge. Somehow it looked very familiar.

"Devilled kidneys!" George exclaimed.

Agnes looked from the cake to the Guardian. "Just how did you manage to get hold of our favourite foods?"

The Guardian gave a slight shrug. "I read your minds. They are your favourites aren't they?"

Agnes nodded as she looked at the cake once again and remembered. It was one she had once made for a special occasion. She had been very proud of it. Not only had she not used any magic in its creation, it had also won first prize at a local flower and produce show. Not only had the Guardian read their minds, it had dipped into their memories. She made a mental note to put a slight screen around herself. The next time the Guardian tried to enter her head he would have to knock. She helped herself to a very large slice. It was just as good as she remembered.

As they sat and ate the ghost of a grey lady drifted through the room It approached the table, walked straight through it and disappeared through the opposite wall.

"I quite like the company." The Guardian remarked.

Agnes helped herself to a glass of wine. "I appreciate that there is no way we can alter the past, but is there any way we can close the portal into the 21st century house?"

"Not if you wish to return." The Guardian replied.

"But we're going back to the 18th century!" Marmaduke remarked. Everyone had noticed how he used a very long and very sharp finger nail to free a bit of sardine from between his teeth.

"If you close it in the 21st century you'll stop it opening in all times." Andrew observed.

Marmaduke turned to face him with a puzzled look on his face. Andrew held a large piece of pineapple and waved it in the air. "Stands to reason. When it appears, it appears in all times, at the same time."

The expression on Marmaduke's face didn't alter. "It's a time thing!" Andrew said as he bit into the pineapple.

Agnes smiled and turned back to the Guardian. "But it will not appear after the 21st century well, after 2015 anyway, am I right?"

"Why 2015?" The Guardian asked.

"Because that was the last time it appeared." She replied.

The Guardian looked towards her. She could see his eyes glowing deep within its cowl. "If that was the last time, I think you have already answered your own question." It replied.

At the far end of the table George let out a slight burp that was the cue for the meal to end. The Guardian clapped his hands and every trace of the food faded away, including the crumbs from the Victoria sponge that had fallen onto Agnes's skirt. Once again they all filed out of the house and walked towards the black shape fastened down at the far side of the gate and wall. The Guardian ducked to one side as a screaming white face flashed over its head and disappeared through the wall of the house.

"They are coming back!" He muttered.

"It is their home." Agnes observed

The Guardian turned towards her. "You know where they come from don't you?"

Agnes nodded. There was a pause.

"So what do we do now?" Marmaduke asked as he peered into the blackness.

Agnes looked at the Guardian "The elemental asked you to make sure we returned to our own place and time."

The Guardian shook its head. "His actual word was assist."

"There's a difference?" Andrew asked, beginning to suspect some sort of trickery.

The Guardian turned to him. "There is a great difference. The words 'make sure' imply I have the ability. 'Assist' means to help you. In this particular usage of the words it means 'help you find your own way back'"

Marmaduke let out a slight snarl. Andrew took a step towards the Guardian. Agnes held her hand up to halt any arguments. "What you really mean is you can't make sure, because you don't know how to."

The Guardian nodded. Agnes continued. "And the fact that you will assist us means you will help us find a way."

The Guardian nodded. "Follow me." It said and stepped into the void. Agnes, Marmaduke and Andrew followed. George remained where he was. He looked across to his motorcar, the Wally was sitting in the front seat."Fancy a ride old chap?" he asked. The Wally nodded its head and clapped its hands. George climbed into the driving seat, started the engine and drove off into the barren landscape.

Chapter Eleven

This time inside the void there was no sensation of falling. Instead they found themselves walking along a strip of pathway that seemed to be suspended inside the void. Agnes looked behind her. There was nothing to be seen. She tried sending out her senses. Nothing happened. The Guardians voice echoed in the emptiness. "Magic does not work on the pathways."

"You mean there's more than one?" Andrew asked.

"Their number is infinite!" The Guardian replied. Somehow that answer didn't give any of them a lot of comfort.

As they were in a timeless place it took no time before a door appeared at the side of the pathway. Agnes looked at it. It looked as if it had once been the doorway to a typical English house of around the 1930's. It had coloured glass set inside a frosted window, a letterbox and a door knocker was underneath it.

The Guardian walked straight on. A second door

appeared, then a third and fourth. Soon they seemed to be walking down a passageway lined with doors. Eventually the Guardian came to a stop in front of a door that seemed to be exactly like all the rest. He put his hand on the handle, opened it and turned to the others.

"Wait!" He said and opened the door. They were met with a scene of glaring white. Snow blew in their faces. A harsh cold wind blew passed them. The Guardian closed the door again.

"Wrong one?" Asked Andrew.

The Guardian started walking down the corridor. "Just checking!" It said without looking around.

They continued passing the series of identical doors. Eventually the Guardian stopped once again. They stood back as he opened it. Cautiously they looked through. It opened onto blue water as far as they could see. It was flat, hardly moving. No waves broke on its surface. A dim sun shone from a pale blue sky. In the far distance they could see some shapes sticking out of the water. Agnes looked closer. It looked suspiciously like the skyline of 21syt century London, where only the tops of the buildings stood proud of the glassy surface. She looked towards the Guardian who just shook his head as he tried to repress a shudder. "Don't ask!" he said as he closed the door. She didn't.

They came to a stop by yet another door. "Third time lucky!" Andrew said.

"Don't bank on it!" Agnes replied.

The Guardian turned to look at her. She stood her ground. "Go on, admit it. You have no idea, you're just hoping to strike lucky."

The Guardian turned back to the door. "I am assisting." It said and opened the door.

They were looking out on a wild landscape. Mountains loomed in the distance under a grey, rain filled sky. Dark clouds hid the sun. A storm was brewing. The ground beneath them was covered in scrub and scattered clumps of trees. As they watched there was a flash of red. A shot rang out and the Guardian fell forwards.

Instinctively Marmaduke dropped on one knee, pulled his pistol out and scanned the landscape. He saw red and pulled the trigger. Andrew dived down and began pulling the Guardian backwards towards the doorway. Agnes moved her arm in a sweeping motion. The air glowed for a second.

"Protection spell!" she announced.

She was just in time. A line of bushes seemed to explode in smoke and a shower of deadly musket balls hit the shield and bounced harmlessly off. From behind them they heard a great roar and a cacophony of sound. She could hear drums beating, bagpipes and chanters wailing. She turned and found she was facing a charge by an army of men dressed in plaid and trews. Many had bare feet and bare legs. Some held swords and bucklers. Some held muskets, all were primed and ready to fire. Another volley of shots exploded out from the bushes. Many of the men at the front of the charge fell. The men behind them jumped over the dead and wounded and continued racing forward. Agnes turned to see Marmaduke helping Andrew drag the Guardian through the doorway. She followed and closed the door behind her.

Andrew lifted the hood from the Guardians head. A round musket ball had embedded itself into the temple. A mechanical eye hung loose, wires could be seen inside the empty socket.

"Can you fix it?" Andrew asked anxiously.

Agnes bent down and examined the damage. "I can try!"

She began to fumble in her pocket and pulled out a small screwdriver and a pair of pliers.

"Are you sure about this?" Andrew asked.

Agnes nodded and moved her empty hand. The screwdriver and pliers seemed to take on a life of their own. They moved over the damage and in and out of the eye socket. They all watched as the tools extracted the musket ball and replaced the mechanical eye, then once they had repaired the damage they simply disappeared.

"He's still not moving!" Marmaduke observed. He bent down and retrieved the musket ball, then held it up and examined it. Suddenly there was a little pop and the thing disappeared, leaving Marmaduke holding nothing.

"It didn't belong here!"Agnes said as she rummaged in her pocket once more. This time she pulled out four AAA batteries.

Andrew looked at the small cylindrical objects as Agnes placed them onto the Guardians chest. The she closed her eyes and moved her hand across them. A blue light flashed from her palm and danced over the batteries and across the Guardians chest. The Guardian gave a jerk and then fell back, inert and silent.

"They work for mechanical bunnies!" She muttered. She tried again. This time the blue light was more intense and covered the Guardians entire body. It gave another jerk, then another. Then it sat up and raised it hand to the damaged eye, pulled it out, turned it around, and reinserted it into its socket.

"Upside down!" The Guardian remarked.

"Mechanical bunnies?" Andrew asked.

"It's a time thing!" Agnes replied.

The Guardian climbed back to its feet. One hand brushed the front of its tunic whilst the other felt for the hole in its head. It wasn't there. He looked at Agnes. "Very good. You have talent."

Agnes shook her head. "I stole the rejuvenation spell from the elemental."

The Guardian continued. "I didn't say it was magic. Stealing anything from an elemental takes
195

great talent." He bent his legs as if testing that they still worked. They did. "Come on!" he said and set off down the corridor once again.

After they had walked a little way Andrew spoke. "What happened back there?"

"The English army were having a battle with a Scots army!" Marmaduke replied.

"When did that happen?" Andrew asked.

"Sometime, someplace. Perhaps it's yet to happen. I've really no idea!" Agnes answered.

Eventually the Guardian stopped at another door and placed his hand on the doorknob. He turned it and very slowly pushed the door open. Everything seemed to be quiet so he opened it wider. In front of them was the upstairs bedroom of the 18th century house. The Guardian opened the door wider and stood to one side allowing them to pass through. Agnes went first. She paused on the threshold and sent out her feelings. At last, they were in the right place at the right time. She stepped forward into the room. Andrew and Marmaduke followed. Once inside they turned around. The black void was behind them. They could see the Guardian standing inside it, hovering in mid air.

"I have assisted. Now I return." It said and then vanished along with the portal.

Agnes moved her finger and a pattern traced itself on the floor where the portal once stood. "Build a wall around it." She said to Andrew. He gave a shrug. "I just buy the timber I've no say in the design of the place."

Agnes sighed. "If you want anything done..." She moved her hands and a solid brick wall appeared in front of her. It was double thickness with a thin gap between the bricks. It divided the room creating two smaller ones. She moved her hands once more and the upstairs of the house rearranged itself. The staircase now led to a small landing that in turn led to three bedrooms.

"Right! That's sorted that!" She turned to Andrew. "If I were you I'd get rid of the timber as soon as possible."

He looked at the wall. "What will the builders say?"

"Don't worry about the builders. I'm sure that

when they arrive in the morning they'll be very pleased with their work they've done so far."

"But...." Andrew was about to say before Agnes cut him off. "It's exactly as the blueprints say it should be."

"But they'll remember not building it!"

"No they won't!" She replied.

As they arrived at the bottom of the stairs Agnes twitched her fingers. Andrew gave a slight jerk and turned towards her.

"Agnes, you gave me a fright." He looked behind her to see Marmaduke standing in the shadows.

"What are you two doing here?"

"I heard you were buying old timbers." She said. Marmaduke raised his eyebrow.

Andrew looked puzzled. "It's a fair deal. They want to sell, the owner wants rid. Everyone benefits."

Agnes gave a smile. "Especially Mr Andrew Chance!"

Andrew had the grace to blush.

"We'll leave you to it!" She said and walked out of the front door.

Andrew gave a puzzled shrug and returned to his task of measuring up the remaining timbers at the foot of the staircase. He looked upstairs, the builders had made a good job of the upper floor. Somehow they had created a third room. He nodded and returned to his measuring.

As they walked down Tuthill towards home Marmaduke turned to Agnes. "He really can't remember anything?"

Agnes stopped. "It was for the best. You know I hate interfering with people's thinking, but it's Andrew. The last thing we need is him inventing the motor car."

Marmaduke grinned. "I see what you mean!"

Later that night as they were sat around the fire Agnes put her cup of tea down. "Right, you stay here. First thing in the morning I'm popping back to the 21st century. Loose ends you know." Marmaduke didn't know.

Chapter Twelve.

The early morning sun was fighting a losing battle
with the grey rain threatening clouds. A left over
dampness was still hanging in the air when a fox
trotted down Tuthill. The policeman standing at
the door of the house stifled a yawn and moved
from one foot to the other..He was hungry, cold
and in dire need of relieving himself. The fox
watched silently from the steps at the end of the
street. Then it twitched its nose. The policeman felt
the pressure on his bladder. He stuck his head out
of the doorway, made sure no one was in sight,
moved further down the street and began to relieve
himself against the wall of the house next door.
The feeling of relief was so great that he closed his
eyes in pleasure. That was why he never noticed
the fox slip into the house and gently and quietly
padded its way upstairs. It paused on the landing
and the air shimmered. Agnes moved her hand and
a shield formed around her body, reflecting light,
making her invisible. She looked at the rooms.
There were only two. She tutted to herself.
Sometime in the past someone had removed her
wall and redesigned the upper floor back to its
original state.

"So that's how the void re-appeared!" she said to herself.

She examined the floorboards where the portal had appeared. There was no trace of anything to suggest it was once there. Now all she had to do was to make sure it could never re-appear. However there was a problem. She couldn't redesign the upper floor and magic a third room right in the middle of a police investigation. Or could she?

She shook her head. No she couldn't. It would drive the police mental. Not only that but they would probably pull it down again just to see how it had appeared. This would take a bit of thinking about. She thought, then she thought again. Then she reached into her pocket and pulled out a selection of herbs and spices. She spread them on the floor where the portal had appeared, and then rummaged in her pocket once again, this time pulling out some old beads, a line of thread, a brown eagle feather and one or two more items that it would be best not to mention, after all this was a very powerful spell.

When she was satisfied she had all the right ingredients she mixed them up in the palm of her hand and then tossed to mixture into the air. The

201

ingredients seemed to float in the air above the herbs and spices. As they hung there the air seemed to shift. There was a flash of soft white light and for a brief second it seemed as if a glass wall had appeared. Then it disappeared. Agnes looked. The room looked just the same as it was before she cast her spell. She rummaged in her pocket once again and pulled out an acorn. Very gently she held it in her hand then tossed it into the room. As it passed through the invisible glass wall there was a very slight shudder and the thing seemed to move fractionally in its flight. Then it fell onto the floorboards and rolled across the wooden floor.

The air shimmered and the fox raced back down the stairs, startling the policeman who had heard the noise and entered the doorway. The speed of the fox passing between his legs caused him to spin. In his alarm he shouted out. As the fox disappeared down the street two more policemen appeared at the opposite end.

"Let them sort that out!" she said to herself.

Just for the sheer perverse pleasure of it when she reached the top of the Custom House Steps the air shimmered. The fox disappeared and an elderly lady appeared. She turned around and retraced her steps into Tuthill. As she approached the police tape she stopped and paused for breath, just like any old lady should after climbing all those steps. In front of her, at the opposite side of the tape were the three policemen. One was pointing in her direction, repeating the word "fox". Another was peering into the building whilst the third was speaking into his radio.

"Good morning gentlemen!" She said with a little wave as she passed them. As she turned towards her own street she heard one of them ask "Where did she come from?" The others ignored him.

Marmaduke and Agnes sat in their respective chairs in their 18th century living room. Marmaduke, having eaten a dish of sardines was dozing. His tea steamed next to him. Agnes was looking into the glowing embers watching a small flame flicker. A lump of coal slid down and crackled as it burst into flames.

Marmaduke woke with a start. He focused his good eye on Agnes."I take it everything has been sorted out?"

"If you mean have I sorted out the portal, yes." Agnes replied.

Marmaduke grunted. Agnes wasn't going to let him get away with that. "Actually I've done something rather ingenious, even if I do say it myself!"

That was the cue for Marmaduke to feign interest. If he was truthful he had no idea of what and how things had happened. All he really understood was that he'd fallen through some sort of hole and ended up in a strange land inhabited by people and things that, now he was home, he really didn't want to meet again. Still he sat up and paid attention.

"I put a spell around the place where the portal appears.When it reappears it will be inside a mirror. That will reflect itself into itself. It will simply vanish into another location."

"Where?" He asked eventually. He had a slight problem working out how something could disappear inside itself.

Agnes gave a shrug of her shoulders. "Wherever it goes next, or wherever it came from." She noticed that Marmaduke's face was blank. "Look, think of a door. You go into a door and come out the other side. You go through the kitchen and come out in the yard, yes?"

204

Marmaduke couldn't argue with that so he nodded. "Well I've just altered where it comes out!" she said.

That was good enough explanation for Marmaduke. Before he could close his eye Agnes continued. "You're probably wondering about George and the screaming heads."

He wasn't but he nodded anyway.

"Well I puzzled about the ghost heads for a long while. Then I realised what they were. They were the ghosts of all the people who had fallen onto the void."

That caught Marmaduke's attention. He shuffled up in his seat and leant forward. "Why didn't it happen to us?" He asked with a slight shudder.

"Because we were invited. We arrived as guests of the elemental. He called us using the Guardian."

"How did the Guardian know where to find you? Come to that how did he know of you in the first place?"

Agnes smiled. "Because sometime in the past, in a different dimension, I had already done the task, and no doubt sometimes in the future, in another dimension, I will do it again."

Marmaduke blinked. The train had gone and he wasn't on it. "I don't understand!" he said.

Agnes shook her head. "Actually, I'm not that sure that I do."

Marmaduke changed the subject. "What about the police investigation?"

Agnes shook her head. "They'll find nothing. Sooner or later someone in authority will decide too much money is being spent. In the days of the 21st century, austerity and cuts to police budgets will make sure that the investigation will be run down. They will simply stop using their resources on it. The case will be left open, but they will stop their investigations. The house will be sold. Some developer will buy it and it will become a holiday home once again."

She stood up. "Come on I fancy a drink and a catch up with the local gossip. Let's go down to the Three Mariners."

As they approached the top of the Dog and Duck steps Marmaduke paused. "What about George?" he asked.

"I've a feeling he'll be fine!" Agnes said as she headed towards the pub.

Epilogue
England 1910

The motor car was pootleling along the road. The driver was sat upright behind the wheel. There was nothing else in sight. The driver looked at the tree lined avenue that formed a green canopy above his head. Suddenly a hole in the road appeared. He slammed on the brake with such a force that he shot forward and banged his head on the windscreen. The knock was so heavy that he passed out so that he didn't see a cowled figure appear out of the hole. It rose and raised a hand and a blue light flashed. It hit the front of the car sending it spinning across the road until it came to rest against the trunk of a tree. Satisfied that the damage was light and that the driver wasn't hurt the Guardian made a move with its hand and disappeared back into the hole.

George woke up and felt the bump on his forehead. He climbed out of the car and examined its front. The bumper was bent and a headlight broken.

"That was a lucky escape." A voice next to him observed.

George looked up to see a little man sat in the passenger seat. "Who are you?" he asked.

"I'm the passenger" The man replied. Then he jumped down and walked to the front of the car. "Come on, let's push and get the old girl back on the road." He said and began pushing the car.

George took off his jacket and pushed. The car rolled backwards into the road. George climbed into the driver's seat as the little man stood at the front of the car and turned the starting handle. It fired up first time. The little man gave a laugh of pleasure and jumped into the passenger seat and the car continued its way along the Banbury to Oxford Road.

END.

ABOUT THE AUTHOR

Graham Rhodes has over 40 years experience in writing scripts, plays, books, articles, and creative outlines. He has created concepts and scripts for broadcast television, audio-visual presentations, computer games, film & video productions, web sites, audio-tape, interactive laser-disc, CD-ROM, animations, conferences, multi-media presentations and theatres. He has created specialised scripts for major corporate clients such as Coca Cola, British Aerospace, British Rail, The Co-operative Bank, Bass, Yorkshire Water, York City Council, Provident Finance, Yorkshire Forward, among many others. His knowledge of history helped in the creation of heritage based programs seen in museums and visitor centres throughout the country. They include The Merseyside Museum, The Jorvik Viking Centre, The Scottish Museum of Antiquities, & The Bar Convent Museum of Church History.

He has written scripts for two broadcast television documentaries, a Yorkshire Television religious series and a Beatrix Potter Documentary for Chameleon Films and has written three film scripts, The Rebel Buccaneer, William and Harold

1066, and Rescue (A story of the Whitby Lifeboat) all currently looking for an interested party.

His stage plays have performed in small venues and pubs throughout Yorkshire. "Rambling Boy" was staged at Newcastle's Live Theatre in 2003, starring Newcastle musician Martin Stephenson, whilst "Chasing the Hard-Backed, Black Beetle" won the best drama award at the Northern Stage of the All England Theatre Festival and was performed at the Ilkley Literature Festival. Other work has received staged readings at The West Yorkshire Playhouse, been short listed at the Drama Association of Wales, and at the Liverpool Lesbian and Gay Film Festival.

He also wrote dialogue and story lines for THQ, one of America's biggest games companies, for "X-Beyond the Frontier" and "Yager" both winners of European Game of the Year Awards, and wrote the dialogue for Alan Hanson's Football Game (Codemasters) and many others.

OTHER BOOKS BY GRAHAM A RHODES

"Footprints in the Mud of Time,
The Alternative Story of York"

"The York Sketch Book."
(a book of his drawings)

"The Jazz Detective."

"The Collected Poems vol 1 1972 – 2016"
"The Collected Poems vol 2 2016 – 2020"
The Collected Poems vol 3 2020 – 2022
(the Covid Years)
"The Collected Poems vol 4 2022 – 2024"

"Poetry
52 years of performance poetry"
An autobiography of poetry gigs and performances

"The View from the Pink Monster"
An autobiography of 70's London

The Agnes the Scarborough Witch Series

"A Witch, Her Cat and a Pirate."

"A Witch, Her Cat and the Ship Wreckers."

"A Witch, Her Cat and the Demon Dogs."

"A Witch, her Cat and a Viking Hoard."

"A Witch, her Cat and TheWhistler."

"A Witch, her Cat and The Vampires."

"A Witch her cat and the Moon People."

"A Witch her Car and a Fire Demon."

"A Witch her Cat And a Revolution."

"A Witch her Cat and an Alchemist.;"

All books by Graham Rhodes can be ordered via Amazon –

https://www.amazon.co.uk/stores/Graham-Rhodes/author/B00JHIW2BQ?

Photographic Books

"A Visual History of York."

"Leeds Visible History"

"Harbourside – Images of Scarborough Harbour"
(A book of photographs available via Blurb)

"Lost Bicycles"
(A book of photographs of deserted and lost
bicycles available via Blurb)

"Trains of The North Yorkshire Moors"
(A Book of photographs of the engines of the
NYMR available via Blurb)

Printed in Great Britain
by Amazon

40630812R00119